PASSION MODEL

PRAISE FOR PASSION MODEL

"Chock full of beloved SF conventions, yet far, far hotter than anything Isaac Asimov or Philip K. Dick ever dared to write. You'll read it in one sitting!"

—Shell Perington

"If you're into erotica and Science Fiction, this is definitely the book for you!"

—Chere Gruver
Sensual Romance Reviews

ALSO BY MEGAN HART

Convicted
Dream Upon Waking
Lonesome Bride
Love Match
Passion Model
Playing The Game

PASSION MODEL

BY

MEGAN HART

AMBER QUILL PRESS, LLC
http://www.amberquill.com

PASSION MODEL
AN AMBER QUILL PRESS BOOK

This book is a work of fiction. All names, characters,
locations, and incidents are products of the author's imagination,
or have been used fictitiously. Any resemblance to actual persons
living or dead, locales, or events is entirely coincidental.

Amber Quill Press, LLC
http://www.amberquill.com

Rating: NC-17

Layout and Formatting provided by: ElementalAlchemy.com

PUBLISHED IN THE UNITED STATES OF AMERICA

To anyone who's ever reached for the stars,
and to my husband David Frank,
without whom none of this
would be possible

CHAPTER 1

The scent of sex is an aphrodisiac for some. For others, a reminder of last night's drunken mistake. For me, it's just part of the job.

The crowd parted before me like the thighs of a LUV 180 at the sight of a twentycredit chit. I passed a number of Pleasurebots, but didn't stop. I'd spotted the one I wanted the minute I walked through the Lovehut door. An early model PSSN-M, maybe an 02 or an 03, one of the first Pleasurebots to strut off the assembly line. A dark-haired one, with dark eyes, instead of the standard blond and blue. The muscled arms and taut abs looked factory issue, but the rest was clearly a custom order.

Pleasurebots don't keep to themselves, but this one stood along the wall, alone. He could have been waiting for someone, but I suspected something more serious, like a malfunction. I made my way through the bumping and grinding crowd, my hand ready to grab my stunner if I needed it. Some PSSNs have a malfunctioning ignition. You can turn them on, you just can't turn them off. A man who rented a PSSN-F-02 in one of the older Lovehuts learned that the hard way. She fucked him to death. Since then, Howard Adar and the Newcity Ruling Council have had the Recreational Intercourse Operatives working heavy duty overtime to find the faulty models and haul them in for repairs. It isn't always easy. There are certain men and women who will pay ten times the going rate for the thrill of risking a Passion Model with a malfunctioning ignition.

It isn't easy to convince a PSSN he or she needs to be fixed, either, not when shoddy repairs can put them out of commission for a long time. Sometimes, even forever. Passion Models can spot an R.I. Op a mile away, even out of uniform. Sometimes they run.

This one met my eyes and let a slow, hot smile cross his perfectly shaped lips like synthetic butter on a hot cob of articorn. "Hello, Officer."

"Operative GMMA 03271971." I slid up my sleeve to show him the tattoo badge on my forearm. "Personal ID unit?"

He spread his fingers in a mock-innocent gesture. "Must have left it at home."

I raised one eyebrow at him to let him know I wasn't fooled. "You know you'll have to come to the nearest inspection station with me."

In the glaring neon light from above the bar, his eyes looked dark as midnight. Blue and green swirls glittered from the flashing lights. He frowned.

"You're kidding me."

"Do I look like I'm kidding?"

He took the opportunity to let his gaze move completely along my body, paying special attention to my nipples, which pushed at the navy blue artisilk of my uniform. And then, damn him, when he looked at the junction of my legs, he licked his lips.

"No, Officer. You don't."

"You know the laws, buddy. All bots have to be registered and licensed…and inspected." This close, he smelled unbelievable. I could smell him even above the tang of deathsticks and hallucinabars. This Passion Model was high class.

He nodded then, but his dark eyes narrowed. "You think I'm—"

I put my hand on my stunner far less than casually. "Are you going to give me a hard time?"

At my unintentional pun, he flashed me that grin again. "I guess I am. If you insist."

I made a show of shaking my head and rolling my eyes, but since it appeared he was going to come with me quietly, I just waved him toward the door. God-of-choice, the view from behind was just as sweet. I've always had a soft spot in my heart for the PSSN-M. They were built with a quality that seems to have gone by the wayside. Sure, the newer Pleasurebots have been improved. They make the PSSY models with an intelligence to rival any sixth grader, and the CUM 180s can even add and subtract. But when it comes right down to their real function, sex, the first PSSNs have a wonderful quality all their own, lost in the later upgrades. A sense of humor. I guess most people don't like to laugh while they're naked.

He tossed a glance over his shoulder as we pushed through the doors to the parking lot. "You sure you want to do this?"

"It's my job, metalboy. Keep it moving."

And did he ever. I hadn't seen an ass move like that since R.I. Op training, when we were forced to undergo hours of simulated stimulation—and even most of the simstim hadn't looked that good.

"Someone put a lot of money into you," I told him.

He paused at the edge of the moving tread sidewalk and gave me another of his cocky grins. "Which way do you want me?"

He was asking me which direction I wanted him to take the pedtread, but his sexy double entendre served its purpose. I felt the flush rise along my cheeks and my nipples strained the navy artisilk of my uniform even further. I was going to enjoy this inspection, faulty ignition or no.

"Follow me."

If we used the pedtread, the nearest inspection station would be only a minute away. Its red neon sign blinked a way for us as we stepped off the pedtread and onto the sidewalk. He looked up at the sign, one of the more graphic ones. This one showed a gigantic erect phallus penetrating a pulsating vagina. The neon was old and flickering, giving the simulated copulation a frenzied look.

He nodded toward it. "In there?"

His pretense at innocence was beginning to annoy me. "You have another place in mind?"

He let that liquid chocolate gaze slide down over my breasts and center between my thighs again before he replied. "My apartment, maybe."

"You know that's illegal. Get inside."

He hesitated again, one foot on the doorstep. "I've never been inside one of these places."

For an instant, just a moment, I felt sorry for him. It's not a Passion Model's fault if he or she malfunctions. Still, the laws had been passed and I was just doing my job. Better for me to risk a bot going into overdrive than an untrained civilian. I could handle it. Most people couldn't.

"Inside."

He shrugged again and laughed. "Sure thing."

The benches in the lobby were empty. All the magazines had been

3

put away neatly in their racks. A pair of saucy breasts peeked out at me from one magazine cover. A set of nice firm male buns showed on another. Directly ahead of us sat the receptionist, and behind her desk stretched the long corridor of inspection rooms.

"Slow night?" I slid up my sleeve to show her the tatbadge, though Miriam and I had known each other since I first graduated from R.I.O.

Miriam nodded and brushed her waist length ebony hair over one shoulder with crimson-painted nails. The movement slid her neckline even farther open to show the cherry tips of her perfect white breasts. Behind me, I heard the PSSN let out a low mutter. Miriam smiled.

"Yeah." She looked me over. "But I might say that you are looking fine tonight, Gemma."

"I'm on duty."

She shrugged. "I'm just saying."

I had to force back a chuckle. "Just sign us in, okay?"

Miriam yawned. "Take your pick. They're all empty."

I held out my arm so she could scan the badge, then opened my eyes so she could give me the retinal scan. The bright light, as always, left dark spots in my vision for a few seconds. Blinking, I stopped her when she moved to give my detainee the scan.

"He doesn't have a license."

A Pleasurebot without a license wouldn't have a retscan code either. Newcity Council's pressure to keep the Lovehuts clean hadn't extended to a bigger budget. Captain Rando was coming down hard on the department for unnecessary expenses, and full scans cost a minimum of .75 credits. I didn't want to be on the Chief's rant list without reason.

Miriam looked at him more closely. "Malfunction?"

I gave him a glance. "No reports and no complaints. Just a random inspection. He didn't have his personal ID unit, so…"

"You have got the best job." Miriam sighed. "C'mon."

Through the entire exchange, my handsome Passion Model had remained silent. When Miriam left the security of her desk, however, he let out a low, strained whistle. I could understand why. Miriam's skirt covered her from waist to toes, but the material was so sheer nothing was hidden. Her taut buttocks were clearly visible under the cloth. When she reached the door to the inspection room, the dark triangle of her pubic area pressed against the gauzy cloth. It was just demure enough to be totally captivating.

"See you later," she said, and gave my bot a wink that made him groan.

Once inside the inspection room, I gave him a moment to calm down. "Have a seat."

Predictably enough, he chose the bed. I stayed standing while I prepared to read him his rights. "You are aware that Mandate 6978 requires all Pleasurebots to be licensed, registered and regularly inspected?"

"Yeah. I know about that."

I fingered the top snap of my jumpsuit. "You are aware that by not providing me with the appropriate license you gave me reason to require you to accompany me to Inspection Station 7308 for a full and thorough inspection of all your functions, to be completed at my discretion and to my satisfaction?"

He ran a hand through his hair, suddenly looking nervous. "Yeah."

"Are you prepared to abide by my decisions regarding your function and ability, should I determine you need repairs?"

Now he laughed. "Sure. Yeah."

"You seem to be taking this awfully lightly," I said. "This is a serious offense."

He forced his smile into a serious look. "Sorry, Officer."

"State your name."

"Declan."

I sighed. "Your ID number?"

He frowned. "I don't think I have one."

Memory wipe. So far he hadn't exhibited any of the tics or tremors that signaled a faulty ignition, but loss of RAM could indicate a bigger problem. "Never mind. I can probably find your registration code."

He laughed again, more loudly. I didn't like his attitude, but I didn't show my annoyance. He'd be begging for mercy when I finished with him, anyway.

"Let's just get started, ok?"

He looked a little nervous again. "What do you want me to do?"

I didn't have to think too hard about that one. "Stand up."

He did.

I reached over and grabbed his belt buckle, then pulled him around until his back was against the wall. I unbuckled his belt and tugged the waist of his pants over his hips. Beneath he wore black drawers, snug against the bulge at his crotch. Along with the dark hair and eyes, it seemed someone had paid for package enhancement, too.

I hooked my thumbs into the elastic. As I went to my knees, I pulled his clothes down all the way. The softness of his dark pubic hair brushed my cheek as I got into position.

"Wait!"

I paused, my mouth almost on the tip of his half-erect penis. "Look, this is my job. You need to be inspected. Don't make it so difficult."

He seemed uncertain what to say. "This is it? You're just going to go down on me?"

I looked up at him. For a lot of women, kneeling in front of a man with his cock ready to go down their throats makes them feel submissive. Dominated. For some, even at risk. Not me. Taking a man's dick in my mouth, aside from being part of the job I was trained to do, is one big power-rush. Nothing quite like it.

"What do you want me to do, Sweetheart? Kiss you first?"

"I just thought…"

"Don't think," I told him. "Just react."

I slid the length of him inside my mouth. In moments, he was completely hard. I tongued the shaft, then let my lips caress the head of his penis. He throbbed against my tongue and let out a moan.

Have I mentioned that I'm very good at my job?

He muttered an expletive. I pinched his thighs lightly in chastisement, but he didn't seem inclined to pull away. Not many did once we got down to business.

I took him further, until the head of his penis nudged the back of my throat. He uttered another muffled curse, this one interspersed with words one usually heard in prayer. I smiled, my mouth curved around him, and I let the length slide back out.

"Good boy," I murmured and patted his thighs again. They were firm, with muscles that now stood out as he leaned against the wall. "You're doing fine."

"I think there's something you need to know," he began, but I shut him up by swirling my tongue around his tip.

When I let him slide back out, I tongued open the hatch on the tiny compartment hidden in my left back molar. I bit down just hard enough to release a few drops of aphrodisiac gel that numbed my tongue but would instantly enhance any sensations this blow job was giving him. I felt him react as the gel coated his shaft.

His hands found my hair. He didn't pull, so I let them stay there. I used one hand to anchor his penis while I moved my mouth, and I unsnapped my jumpsuit with the other. I slipped my hand down between my thighs to turn myself on.

As always, that first electric jolt as my finger pressed my sexbutton had me shuddering with instant pleasure. A tiny sigh escaped me. I was ready to move on with the inspection.

"I'm going to lay down on the bed, and you're going to orally stimulate me until orgasm, or to cease upon my command," I said, still kneeling. He couldn't know it would be nearly impossible for him to make me come. I could hold out for as long as it took for a faulty ignition to malfunction. Orgasms are for private life, not for work.

Declan's thighs clenched, his erection bobbed. He'd taken his hands from my head and now he fisted them at his sides. I watched his face for any unusual reactions. "Got it?"

He nodded and swallowed. I watched the way his throat worked, the way his tongue swiped across his mouth, and felt an answering tingle between my legs. He was ready, all right. Turned on and ready to do what he'd been made to do.

"Can I touch you?"

His question was so sweet it made me pause in stripping off my uniform. I looked at him curiously. "I'd say you're going to have to. You have a problem?"

He shook his head and ran his hands through his dark hair, making it stand up in spikes. I noticed he had an off-center widow's peak. His hairline made a jagged point on the left side of his forehead. Unusual to find a Pleasurebot with asymmetrical features....

Before I could ponder further, he'd stepped up to me and crushed his mouth to mine. I stand five-foot-ten and weigh a good 140 pounds, all muscle, so I'm no wilting flower. He'd taken me by surprise, though, and I don't like that. I stepped down, hard, and the heel of my boot crunched on his toe.

He yelped and jumped away. "What the hell?"

"You're not good at following instructions, are you?" Keeping my eyes on him, I bent to pick up the puddled artisilk of my jumpsuit. I pulled the stunner from my utility belt and held it out. "Kissing isn't allowed."

He wiped his mouth with the back of one hand and seemed ready to say something. Instead, he just nodded. "Sorry."

"Do I need to repeat the instructions?"

"No."

"Good." I kept the stunner with me and moved toward the bed.

I enjoyed watching his eyes widen as I lowered myself back onto the pillows. Inspection station beds aren't equipped with fancy comforters and blankets—they're made for fucking, not sleeping. But every one always has a full complement of pillows, helpful to aiding any sexual position required. I scooted back against the headboard, my head propped up and my legs spread wide.

"I'll be testing your reactions to sexual stimuli while in performance mode," I explained to him. I know I sounded matter of fact, but the fact of the matter was that my sex had begun to throb. My nipples, too. My training from the Academy conditioned me to respond to sex as well as most of these Pleasurebots. Better, in fact, than some of them. The difference is, Pleasurebots are designed to achieve frequent and swift orgasm. R.I.Ops are trained to resist climax, so we can concentrate on our jobs. They don't call us the Blue Ball Squad because of the color of our uniforms. Lots of Newcitizens think the extra rank and privileges make up for rarely getting to come, and there are times when I agree. Tonight would not be one of them.

He stared at me. "Listen. I really have to tell you something."

"Oh, God-of-choice! You're not a reconditioned model, are you?" The pieces began to fit together. The upgrades on the hair and features, the enhanced package, the memory wipe. This guy must have been through the wringer. "You *have* done this before, right?"

"Yeah, of course, but—"

"Then get up on the bed and do it." I was losing patience by that time. "I don't have all night."

He set his mouth in a thin, grim line. "You're a real hardass, aren't you? Always have to be in charge?"

I've been insulted worse, plenty of times, but for some reason his words stung. I tried not to let it show in my eyes or my voice when I replied. R.I.Ops don't have the luxury of emotion.

"I *am* always in charge."

"Not this time, baby."

Now I was angry. "Watch your mouth, or I might just haul you to the shop."

Then he gave me that grin again, that damned cocky grin which shot fire between my thighs. I narrowed my eyes but couldn't stop the twitch of my hips. He saw it, too, and grinned wider.

He unbuttoned his shirt. "I'll be ready in a minute."

"There's no need for you to fully disrobe." Damn, he looked fine. I concentrated on the series of images which usually worked to keep me focused. A key, a star, a red ball. They weren't working.

The shirt came off to reveal smooth, tan skin. Perfect nipples like two dark coins, surrounded by crinkly hair. More hair furred his chest and ran in a straight, thick line down past his navel and met his thatch of dark pubic hair.

His cock rose proudly from the dark nest. His erection hadn't wilted at all. In fact, when I shifted on the bed to flash him some pink, it twitched in reaction.

"I function better when I'm naked. Besides," he pointed out, "you're naked. Doesn't seem fair."

"It's not protocol."

He shrugged and stepped out of his drawers. "Too late now."

"You're really testing my patience, Declan."

The bed dipped under his weight as he crawled up on it. "Sorry."

He wasn't sorry. I could hear it in his tone of voice. But as his tongue found my clit, I found I didn't really care.

My job is to test these bots to see if their systems are still working all right. The problem is it can take a variety of stimuli to trigger that malfunction. Sometimes it can take hours before a bot reaches that point. For the first time since my rookie days I wasn't sure I could last long enough.

He didn't immediately drill me with his tongue. Instead, he began with a series of soft kisses that tickled my thighs and made me squirm. His hands found my hips and held me still. I let him. His comments about my having to always be in charge still echoed in my head, interfering with the sensation of his mouth on my clitoris. I forced them away and concentrated on his technique.

Declan licked me slowly. Gently, but with enough force behind his mouth to make me wiggle. I felt every breath, every caress. His hands left my hips to stroke my thighs and calves, to wander across my belly. He was good. He was top of the line, no doubt about it. Too soon to tell if he had the faulty ignition, but I had all the time in the world.

"Put your finger inside me," I whispered, and he complied.

I was so wet already; his finger slid inside me like he'd coated it in oil. His tongue danced on my swollen clitoris and urged me toward orgasm. I spread my legs wider to give him more access and gave myself up to the sensation.

He slipped another finger inside me while he suckled gently on my lips and clit. I slid my hands up to my breasts to tug on my nipples. They were iron hard and swollen, just aching for his mouth on them. I had to switch or I'd go over the edge.

"Come up here." He didn't move, instead continuing to focus his attention on my crotch. I tapped his head until he looked up. "C'mon.

9

Up."

He slid up the bed toward me, angling for my mouth again. I held up my hand. "No kissing. Didn't you learn anything?"

He didn't look chastised. "Sorry."

I got up on one elbow to look him in the eyes. "You're not a very good bot, are you?"

He gave me that naughty grin. "Nope."

I shook my head, but a grin tugged at the corners of my mouth. Despite his poor attitude, I was beginning to like Declan.

"Lick my breasts."

He bent his head. "If you insist."

I was beginning to think I'd been wrong. Declan might not have had his license up to date, but he didn't seem to be malfunctioning in any way. I could just force him into coming and let it go at that. Get back to my rounds at the Lovehuts and listen to people whispering behind my back as I passed by. Somehow, that choice didn't sound appealing. Not when I had a very handsome, very hard bot in bed with me.

He mouthed my nipple and took the tiny bud of flesh tenderly between his lips. I relaxed against the pillows, letting him do what he wanted. Passion Models are good about taking the initiative. You might pay more for the privilege, but if you've ever been with a FCK 75 or the COK 187, you find it's worth it. Despite Declan's accusation that I always like to be in control, I find telling my sexual partner how to perform, step-by-step, unfulfilling and tiresome.

He traced the faint flush blooming on my chest and the swell of my breasts. "You're beautiful."

"Flattery will get you nowhere."

He shook his head and bent back to my nipples, sucking on first one and then the other, alternating in perfect rhythm. Without my having to ask, he slipped one hand down between my legs.

He had no trouble finding my erect clit. "You're so wet."

"That means you're doing your job."

He stroked me lightly and smiled when I twitched beneath his touch. "And you're just doing yours."

"Someone"—I paused to take a deep breath against the sensations sweeping through me—"has to keep society safe."

He rolled on top of me and his cock nudged my entrance. "I assume I'm allowed to fuck you now?"

"Show me what you've got."

He slid that thick length inside me and waited a moment, eyes closed, before moving. His weight on me was not unpleasant. Nothing about being with him was unpleasant, actually. I was enjoying this encounter far more than I usually did. I lifted my hips, urging him on.

"I can't tell if your ignition is faulty if you don't perform."

He opened his eyes. "My ignition isn't faulty."

I didn't bother to reply. They never admit to malfunction. I put my hands on his hips, liking the smooth feeling of his skin, then curved my fingers around the furry mound of his buttocks. I stroked his ass as he pumped slowly in and out of me. With every thrust my engorged clit rubbed against his pubic bone. We fit together perfectly, seamlessly.

He bent his head to nip at my throat, and I let his kisses slide. As long as he didn't try and put his lips on mine, I could ignore protocol and procedure, especially since he was so skilled in everything else.

"Are you all like this?" He asked in a whisper against my ear. "Or just you."

I couldn't figure out why he insisted on talking. I didn't answer. I could tell by the way he was speeding up his thrusts that he was close to coming, and I was right there along with him. I pushed his face toward my breasts, biting back a gasp when he found them.

I hooked my legs around the back of his calves, urging him to fuck me harder. Faster. So far he'd shown no signs of breaking rhythm, no erratic behavior.

"Let go," he muttered. "Gemma, I want to make you come."

His words sent me closer to the edge than even his tongue had. When was the last time someone had said that to me? It had been way too long.

I tried to focus on what he was doing rather than what he was saying, but the words kept coming.

"You're so beautiful, Gemma. I want to make you feel good. I want to fuck you until you come. Come with me, please."

I wanted to tell him to shut up, that he was confusing me, but the pleasure arcing through me was too intense. I couldn't speak without moaning. He was sweeping me away, and I didn't care.

"Come with me," he whispered again and gave a little twisting thrust that ground him deliciously against my center again.

Now it was my turn to mutter a curse. I didn't want to see his face, couldn't look into his eyes. His hands on me, his mouth on me, his dick inside me, all were leading to an explosion of feeling I didn't want and couldn't refuse.

He whispered his plea again, and added another. "Look at me.

Please, Gemma."

Was it because he said my name like a lover would, all soft and tender? Was it because he was the first bot to bring me this close to orgasm since I'd been a rookie just out of training? I don't know what made me respond, but I did. I opened my eyes and met his gaze.

"Declan." His name popped out of my mouth before I could stop it, and he groaned at the sound of it.

The shift happened, that tiny instant when the body goes from pleasure to ecstasy. I was going to come, and come hard.

"Fuck me," I managed to say though I wanted only to groan. "Please. I'm going to…"

I didn't have time to finish because the first burning arcs of electric orgasm ripped through me. I'm sure I cried out, made some sort of agonized noise. I pulled him to me, feeling the full length of him sliding in and out, driving into me, making me wet, making me scream, making me come.

I couldn't close my eyes, had to keep them locked on his. Watching him, seeing the way he bit his lip as his own orgasm built and exploded.

Tiny beads of sweat had burst out on his brow and upper lip, and he slid out his tongue to lick them away. My fingers tightened on his shoulders, hard enough to make him protest. I was helpless against the raging force of my climax, but even as it tore through me, I had to speak.

"You're a man!"

He burst inside me, his cock throbbing with a final thrust that sent one last round of sensation jolting through my quivering vagina. I fought the orgasm but lost and could only surrender to it. He buried his head in the curve of my shoulder, and his body shuddered while he gasped out my name again.

Pleasurebots don't sweat. Declan was no Passion Model. He was a real man.

Now his weight held me down, and I shoved him off. My heart pounded with different purpose, and the stars flashing in front of my eyes had nothing to do with my body's reaction to my recent orgasm.

"It's illegal for a Recreational Intercourse Operative to engage in intercourse with a human being while on duty." My voice was hoarse. This man had just given me the best sex I could remember having…and perhaps he'd just cost me my job.

He gave me a lazy grin, apparently not noticing how upset I really was. "I tried to tell you."

I got up from the bed and stalked to the bureau. The slow, hot gush of his seed trickling from my womb stopped me. Pleasurebots don't ejaculate. I wasn't prepared for this. I grabbed one of the towels from the bureau and pressed it to the flow of warm semen. The musky scent of it perked my nipples and made my clit twitch in response.

"Why? Why would you do this?" Keeping my voice calm was a struggle. I'd have to make a report, explain my actions. Would Captain Rando believe I really hadn't seen Declan was a human and not a bot? I'd be sent for reconditioning to update my skills....

"Hey, it wasn't so bad, was it? I thought you enjoyed it."

The sound of that grin in his voice made me whirl around on him. "You jerk! Do you know what you've done? You've jeopardized my career! Do you know what happens to Operatives who fornicate with humans while on duty?"

He sat up and frowned. "Hey, wait, I'm sorry—"

"It's too late to be sorry," I hissed. I threw the towel to the floor, thought better of it, and folded it up. I'd have to take it with me. If Miriam found a come-soaked towel, she'd have to report me.

He watched as I stepped back into my uniform. "I won't tell anybody what happened."

"Shut up," I whispered. "Do you think that will help? I'm in deep shit, and it's all your fault!"

"My fault?" He swung his legs over the bed and gathered up his own clothes. "You're the one who accosted me in the Lovehut. I was minding my own business."

"You should have told me right away you were not a Pleasurebot."

He raised an eyebrow. "You didn't want to hear anything I had to say, remember?"

My cheeks burned. "Get out of here."

He pulled his pants up to his waist, then shrugged into his shirt and stepped into his shoes. "You're not the only one who'd get into trouble, Gemma. I'd get arrested, too."

"That doesn't make me feel any better."

"I won't say anything. I promise!"

I gave him a look as fierce as if I'd threatened him with my stunner. "Get out!"

He opened his mouth to speak, then shut it without saying anything. He went to the door. I watched him go and suddenly felt the taste of his cock in my mouth again.

"Why?" I whispered to his back.

He looked over his shoulder. "I've always had a thing for the XTC 90."

Then he was gone. The door shut behind him with a dry click that made me jump. I reached down between my legs and turned myself off.

stir

CHAPTER 2

"Reports?" Eddie asked me as he came by my cubicle. "I'm heading over to Rando's office if you have any to drop off."

I shook my head and avoided his glance. "Not quite finished yet."

Eddie leaned against the cubicle wall and looked over my shoulder at my monitor. "Rough night?"

"You could say that."

He made a sympathetic noise. "Gang bang?"

I twirled on my chair to look at him and couldn't hold back a laugh. "No. Sorry to disappoint you."

Eddie tapped his portable view screen against one muscled thigh. "You look like hell. Something must have happened."

"I didn't sleep much last night." I turned back to my computer and tried to type in another sentence, but my fingers kept messing up the keys.

I wasn't fooling Eddie. "Gemma, you only need about 45 minutes of sleep a night."

"So, I didn't get it." I hadn't, that was no lie. After my escapade with Declan, I'd gone back out on patrol for another three hours. The result of the overtime hours would look good in my credit account at the end of the month, but I was paying for that time today.

Eddie lowered his voice and moved a little closer. "Need some time in the simstim chamber? I'll trade you my hour this week for a couple of dining credits."

It had to be something serious if Eddie was willing to give up his ₐime for food. "Who is she?"

Eddie sat on the extra chair and stretched out his long legs. My sometime partner was every inch a male, broad shouldered, well-built, lean. Deep golden hair, twinkling blue eyes. In a word, gorgeous. He'd been only minimally altered, too. Night vision, extra stamina, and the standard R.I. Op enhancements like the aphrodisiac gel in his tooth.

"Somebody I met a couple weeks ago."

"Some body or some bot?" I raised a brow at him.

"Fleshgirl this time." Eddie grinned. "Her name's Charlene."

"And you want to take her out to dinner to a nice place." For a minute, I envied Eddie his easy humanity and active social life. But only for a minute. The choice between staying human or turning mecho had been taken from me a long time ago, and there was no use bemoaning it now. The emergicrew who'd found me after the speeder accident had done a fine job, and so had the staff at the surgical hospital. I'd rather be alive than dead.

"Earth to Gemma," Eddie waved a hand in front of my face. "You in there?"

"Sorry. Just…zoning."

Eddie frowned. "God-of-choice, you really did take a hit last night. What happened, G?"

My tiny cubicle didn't have the privacy I wanted, but I leaned closer to him anyway. "When's the last time you had to fill out a IIP form?"

IIP. Incorrectly Identified Pleasurebot. Eddie let out a curse.

"Not for a long time. What happened?"

I shrugged. "He looked like a PSSN-M-02 to me, Eddie. He didn't have a license. He didn't tell me he was a fleshboy until after."

Eddie scrubbed his face and ran his hand back through his hair. "Shit. Why not?"

"He said he had a thing for the XTC 90." I thought of Declan's fingers inside me and his tongue stroking my clit. My heart thudded.

"But you're not—'

"I know. But I'm close enough." I was a few organs beyond being a real XTC 90, but Declan wouldn't have known that. "It gets worse."

Eddie's lush mouth had sent many women, flesh and metal, over the edge into ecstasy. Now he used it to frown at me. "The bastard didn't rape you, did he?"

"Hell no," I said. "Shit, Eddie, you think I couldn't fight off a fleshboy if I had to?"

"Then what?" Eddie took my hand in a gesture so tender it made me want to cry. "What did he do to you, G?"

Eddie was a good partner and a good friend. We'd had our share of adventures on duty and sometimes, even in bed. Eddie was the man who'd shown me how to use my enhanced functions after I came out of rehab and was assigned to the R.I.O. Academy. He'd been my first lover after the accident. If I could share my dirty secret with anyone, it would be Eddie.

"He made me come," I said in a low voice.

Eddie's fingers closed convulsively on mine. "Shit."

"Yeah."

"Rando is going to shit bricks, G."

I let go of Eddie's hand and turned back to my computer. "I'm not going to tell her."

"And that guy isn't going to tell anyone either, right?" Eddie snorted. "He bangs an Op and makes her cream, and he's not going to brag about it?"

"It's a federal offense for him, too, and he knows it." I tapped some more keys and spewed more gibberish onto the screen. "He won't tell."

"How'd it happen?" Eddie's voice was quiet. "You've been working too hard lately. You need a break."

"That's no excuse."

"Rando will suspend you. Dock your pay. Maybe even—"

"Don't say it, Eddie. I know."

Eddie let out low whistle. "Damn, G."

I turned back to give him a smile I didn't feel. "I'll be all right, Eddie. Rando will never find out, and it won't happen again."

He nodded. "I know."

"Give me your stim-time. You can have my extra dining credits." I wouldn't need them. I hate eating in restaurants alone.

Eddie reached over and gave my shoulder a squeeze. "Thanks, G."

He smelled so good that all at once I leaned forward to kiss him. His lips parted beneath mine in automatic response, and I felt the dart of his tongue in my mouth. He tasted like mint. Delicious.

Eddie reached up to cup my breast through the silk of my uniform. His thumb rubbed across my nipple, making it iron hard in seconds. I sighed and broke the kiss before the ache in my crotch could get any deeper.

"You still got it." Eddie shifted so I could see the bulge of his erection.

"Yeah, I know." We grinned at each other, two old friends. "Get out of here."

I tilted my head to watch his ass work as he walked away, then turned back to my computer. Not surprisingly, I couldn't concentrate any longer. The kiss I'd given Eddie had my system revved up, and I couldn't stop thinking about Declan fucking me to orgasm. I needed some stim-time after all.

* * *

With the extra stim-time credits from Eddie on my account, I could spend as much time as I wanted in the room. I punched in 45 minutes on the keypad, and the door hissed shut behind me. I slid out of my uniform and hung it on the hook. I set my boots and belt on the shelf. Naked, I sat on the edge of the cushioned cot that was the room's only furniture.

"Holo on."

The white walls and floor shimmered around me. "Activate program 31."

"Records show program customization. Proceed?" The modulated computer voice asked.

I nodded, as I invariably did, even though I knew I was talking to a machine, not a person. "Fine."

"Customization beginning."

In another moment the shimmering walls and floor solidified. I was in a café. I wore a light dress of some summery fabric that didn't really solidify unless I looked directly at it. I sat at a small table on a balcony overlooking the ocean, a blue ocean, which never failed to make me smile. Earth's one remaining ocean varies in color from red to brown because of the algae farms that provide 90% of the world's food. The blue ocean was a touch of whimsy I'd added after seeing a picture in a history holo once.

My mind told me none of this was real, but it was easy enough to believe my eyes, my nose, my ears, my sense of touch. My mind could tell me I sat naked, alone in a white room on a padded platform, but my body told me a different and more interesting story.

"I'm glad you came today." The man who sat down across from me gave me a smile that seemed genuine enough—if you didn't know he wasn't real. "I've missed you."

Holograms can't be glad, and they can't miss people. All the same, I returned his smile. "Thanks, Nick."

"No tea today?"

18

I looked down at my empty cup, faintly surprised. Usually the program took care of things like that. "I guess not. Maybe it's a glitch."

Nick stood, his handsome face pulled into a gesture of concern. "I'll check it out for you."

I reached for his hand. "Don't worry about it. I don't want tea today, anyway."

He felt solid beneath my fingers. Real. I turned his palm over to stroke the back of his hand, marveling as always at the feeling of hair tickling my fingers.

"I think I know what you do want." Nick tugged my hand hard enough to urge me to stand. Without my boots on, my head came only to his chin. I liked that. I liked him, even if he was only a computer generated fantasy.

"You always do."

Nick's mouth closed on mine. In this program, he always took the lead. It was nice to not have to be the one in charge. He put his arms around me, and his fingers stroked my skin through the wispy dress. I opened my mouth to him, and his tongue darted between my lips.

"The ocean looks so blue today," he murmured. "Like your eyes."

I stopped, again faintly surprised. "You never noticed my eyes before."

"Maybe you never wanted me to notice them before." Nick stroked the hair away from my forehead and ran a finger down my cheek. "I like your hair this color."

I stepped out of his embrace, startled. "It's violet. The same color it's been for months."

He nodded and grinned. "I like it."

"Halt program!"

"Is something wrong?" asked the computer.

I looked around the white room. Nick, the café, the ocean, all had vanished at my command. "Run diagnostics."

A faint whirring sound whispered around me, and the computer spoke again. "Diagnostics complete. What is your malfunction?"

"My holo partner is acting strangely."

"Essex Corporation can not be responsible for customized programs. All customized program actions are triggered by subconscious commands linked directly to your specific brain wave function, as it is recorded in our files. Should you believe your program to be malfunctioning, please contact—"

"I know all that." I ran my hands over my breasts and shivered at the way touching my nipples reverberated in between my legs. I was horny as hell and had to do something about it.

Declan's face flashed in my mind, and I muttered a curse.

"Command not recognized," said the computer. "Proceed with program?"

"Yes. Go ahead."

The wall shimmered again, and Nick's face appeared before mine. The balcony, the face, the ocean all appeared too, exactly where they'd been when I'd halted the program.

"I'm glad you came today," Nick said. "I missed you."

I didn't bother with preliminaries this time. "Kiss me."

Nick was always happy to oblige. Frankly, he wasn't programmed to refuse. He dipped his head to mine and captured my mouth again. He put his hands on my hips, then slid them up to cup my breasts. He ran his thumb across my nipples, all the while kissing me. Kissing me.

His tongue felt so good in my mouth, loving my mouth the way he'd soon love the rest of me. Kissing was a treat, a pleasure, something special and usually forbidden. I might fuck a dozen men or women in one shift's time, I might have every orifice filled over and over, but I never, ever kissed them. Kissing Nick got me so hot, so fast.

He pushed me against the waist high stone wall and ran his tongue along the curve of my jaw, down my neck. He took one nipple in his mouth and suckled it until I cried out. Then he took the other one.

The dress was gone, no longer needed and definitely not wanted. I was naked, exposed to the wind and the sun and scent of the long dead sea. A breeze, triggered by my subconscious command, blew over the wet spot his mouth left.

I supported myself against the wall with nothing but air behind me, yet I had no fear of falling. I closed my eyes to open myself to the sensations. A gull cried. The waves pounded. Nick kissed his way down my body until he found my center.

I buried my hands in his hair as he put his mouth to me there. I felt his hands on my thighs, urging them to part. I had to brace myself on the wall, and the rough stones scratched my flesh as my fingers tightened when he licked me for the first time.

"That's good." My voice didn't sound like my own. I didn't care. Nick didn't care.

He pressed his thumbs on either side of my already pulsing clit, isolating the button of flesh from the rest of my vagina. His tongue made slow, lazy circles there, firm but delicate strokes, and I began to melt. He kept a rhythm going, slow, but steady.

I spread my legs wider and leaned further back over the abyss. All that anchored me to the ground was Nick's hands and his tongue, licking me, stroking me, fucking me. He paused to blow a puff of air across my wet heat, cooling it.

Declan had done that. I didn't want to think of him, but his face filled my mind anyway. I was too far gone, too close to coming to force it away.

Nick's hands became Declan's hands, his mouth Declan's mouth. Declan's tongue licked at my swollen bud, and his finger slipped inside me.

"More," I said. With my eyes closed, nothing seemed quite real. Nothing was real, and I didn't care. It felt too good.

He slid another finger inside me, opening them to stretch me. I moaned. He slid his tongue in feathery strokes down from clit along my labia, and replaced his fingers inside my slit.

I cried Declan's name, not worried I might hurt Nick's feelings. The breeze swept over us, tangling my hair, caressing my body in all the places his hands couldn't reach. The pounding of the waves became the pounding of my heart, a cacophony of white noise that buzzed in my ears.

I didn't have to tell Nick it was time to let me come. With Declan's face and hands and tongue in my head, I only needed the thought of his cock to finish me off.

I remembered the salty, musky taste of him, and I came.

I made a wordless, moaning cry as the good feeling burst through me. It radiated from my anus, through my inner walls and exploded from my clitoris. My vagina bore down on Nick's tongue, clenching and releasing even as he thrust into me harder. I was coming so hard I didn't even need direct stimulation on my clit.

Declan was fucking me. The man who had made me come the night before, the first man to have done so in ages. The man I wanted to be fucking me, sliding his mouth up my body even as I continued to twitch in the last spasms of climax. The man I wanted to kiss me with the taste of me still on his tongue.

I couldn't open my eyes. Couldn't see Nick, who wasn't real. Without looking at him or speaking, I turned until I faced the sea.

The stone wall nudged my stomach and felt cold against my aroused heat. I spread my legs and leaned over the wall, offering myself to Declan's cock.

He pushed into me, the thickness of him like a rod of iron after the soft flexibility of his tongue. I said his name again, in a whisper this time.

"Declan."

He put his hands on my hips to steady his thrusts. He didn't pound me, nor did he tease. He just fucked me, steady and slow, then faster. Just the way I wanted it. Needed it. Craved it.

My orgasm built again, though slower this time. I clutched the stone wall. Strands of my violet hair fell across my face and obscured my vision of the ocean. I tossed them away. I wanted to see my whimsy.

He put one hand on my shoulder and kept the other on my hip. His thrusting became a little ragged, a little sporadic. His breathing told me he was getting close. I wasn't close enough.

"Stroke my clit." I whispered the words, not ordered.

He took his hand from my hip and rested his fingers on my clitoris. I jumped at the contact. Just his direct touch on my sensitized flesh had me tumbling toward climax again.

He thrust, and he stroked in perfect counterpoint. I bent low over the wall, my hair falling into empty space, my eyes wide.

He thrust again, one last time, and my orgasm burst through me. I said his name one last time. I came that way, calling his name and staring at the sea I'd created.

*   *   *

"Gemma, my office. Now." Captain Rando didn't bother with pleasantries even when she was in a good mood. Judging by the look on her face, today wasn't one of those days.

Usually I left the stimroom feeling relaxed and with my mind calm. Not this time. Though I'd experienced two explosive orgasms, my body still tingled with unsatisfied longings. Declan's face in my head left me uncomfortable and jumpy.

Rando jerked her thumb at the silver colored orb on her desk. "This was delivered here for you half an hour ago."

I forced my fingers not to tremble as I lifted the lightweight plastic ball and pressed the button on its side. With a small whirring sound a tiny slit opened in the top. The next instant the image of twelve perfect red roses was projected from the orb. They looked real, even down to the drops of dew on the petals, and a second later, the delicious scent of roses wafted to my nose.

"Someone paid a lot of money for those." Rando rocked back in her chair. "No card. Any idea who your secret admirer might be?"

I kept my face impassive as I shrugged, but my heart began to thud like an out of control Mohanian drum band. "No, sir, I don't."

Rando crossed her arms over her ample chest and frowned. "Boyfriend?"

"No."

"Girlfriend?"

I shook my head. "No, sir."

"Gemma—" Rando sighed, and her fierce demeanor softened for a minute. "How long have you been with R.I.O?"

I didn't even have to think. "Six years, seven months, two weeks, three days."

"That just shows me your internal clock is set." Rando gave me a penetrating look. "In all that time, I've never known you to take a lover."

"No time for it, sir." I pushed the flower orb's button and the flowers disappeared.

"It's not against department policy. As long as you keep it off duty, you can date whoever you like. Even get married." Rando lifted the square viewscreen so I could see my own name flashing there. "You've had an exemplary record, Gemma."

"Thank you." I knew what was coming next, and I braced myself for it.

"There's been some reports of Ops making assignations during duty. Using the inspection stations for dates, that sort of thing."

"I've heard the same rumors, sir."

"You know that can't be allowed." Rando punched in a command, and the viddy screen filled with a familiar face. "Howard Adar's been whipping the Ruling Council into a frenzy about misuse of Pleasurebots, Newcity funds, and a bunch of other crap I don't even want to think about."

Howard Adar spoke directly to the camera, his words coming on the tale of Rando's speech. "I'm not saying they have no rights. But let's ask ourselves, who can we trust? Bots are made to work and serve, they're not given brains to think. Humans are born with the ability to reason and think. But what about those who—"

She hit the mute button and shook her head. "You know what I'm talking about. You haven't filed a report on your last dutytime. Is there anything you'd like to tell me?"

I shook my head, which had begun to pound in time with my heartbeat. "I'll have it on your desk within the hour, Captain."

"Gemma." Rando pointed to the florb I clutched. "If something did happen to any of my Ops while they were on duty, it's my responsibility to take appropriate action. Even if I don't want to. The mandate has come down from the top office. We have an epidemic of malfunctioning Passion Models out there, and the death toll is rising. Not to mention the other myriad of bot problems the factories can't seem to fix. We can't afford to have Ops using dutytime to get off. We don't have the luxury of making mistakes."

"I understand, Captain." I understood, all right. If Rando found out I'd let myself be seduced by a fleshboy while on duty, it wouldn't matter whether or not I'd done it on purpose.

Rando used the stylus to scroll through my file. She looked at me again over the tops of the glasses she kept for show, not need, since laser surgery had become standard requirement to be part of R.I.O. Even through the lenses, her gaze burned me.

"Gemma, when's the last time you took a day off?"

"Day 5 is my usual day off, Sir."

Rando made a noise in her throat. "Shows here you punched in on Day 5. And the Day 5 before that, too."

I studied the florb in my hands. "I had to follow up on a case."

Rando sighed. "Gemma. It's not illegal for you to take some time off. Your records show you haven't even taken your allotted vacay. You get three weeks now. Why?

I shrugged. "No place to go."

"In six whole years?" Rando rapped her knuckles on the desktop. "Surely some place has tempted you. Solaria? Aquafier?"

She'd named two of the hottest vacay spots within warpjump range. "No, sir. I like it here."

"On Earth."

"Yes."

She looked like she might want to say something else, but didn't. "Dismissed."

I thanked her and left the room, carrying the florb away from my body like it might explode if I touched it. When I got to my cubicle, I tossed it in the can, but hesitated before pushing the button which would evaporate it. For reasons I couldn't explain and didn't want to think about, I pulled it back out and slipped it into my shoulder bag.

I finished typing the report, surprised at how easily the lies flew from my fingers and onto the computer screen. Must have been the stim-time. I E'd it to Rando, then sat back in my chair.

The report wasn't my only foray into untruth today. I'd also lied when I told Captain Rando I didn't want to go anywhere. There were, in fact, days when the stink of exhaust and haze-covered sky had me wanting to scream. Days when the taste of man-made water choked me. I wanted to get away, for awhile, to see a clear sky and warm sun, to put my feet in warm sand. To see a real ocean.

I couldn't. I'd been on vacay on Solaria when the accident happened. One minute I'd been speeding along a dry sand road, the next thing I knew, I woke up in hospital with a body that looked like something from a factory that had gone out of business. I couldn't go to any of those places again, those places where smiling waitrons kept bringing free pills and drinks, and one second of misplaced attention could end your life.

Before the accident, I'd worked in one of the big plaza mansions that ringed the city. I was a personal hygiene coordinator for one of the residents, one of the wealthiest old men on the planet. I was entirely responsible for his daily body care, from running his bath at exactly the right temperature to choosing the flavor of toothpaste that would complement the day's planned activities. Once I arrived at the job, I never had to leave the bathroom.

I was good at what I did, and I was paid well. And more importantly, I enjoyed it. I liked Alfie Zoydman, my employer, and his fetish for fresh breath.

I'd even, for a very short time, been married. Steve had never come to see me in the hospital. I'd received the notice from his lawyer during my recovery.

Not a divorce notice. A dissolution notice, instead. He had every right, since I'd been declared legally dead, to dissolve our union. His claim that I was not the woman he'd married stood firm. I wasn't. Several pounds of wire, batteries and artificial organs proved that. More than fifty percent of my body's systems and/or parts had been replaced. I was mecho.

Dissolution meant I wasn't entitled to take with me anything we'd gained or created together during the marriage. That I might be left destitute obviously hadn't bothered my former husband.

I'd spoken to him only once since then. "I'm still the same person, Steve."

"No." His voice sounded tinny through the speaker, and he refused to meet my eyes through the screen. "No, you're not."

What Steve didn't seem to realize, and his lawyer to care, was they hadn't replaced all my organs. Some of them were still mine. Including my heart.

CHAPTER 3

I left the office still buzzing with tension. Stim-time hadn't relaxed me enough. I needed a workout. I hopped a pedtread and mingled elbow to elbow with the crowd.

There's something so sensual about the crush of humanity. I don't mean sexual, which is something else entirely. Sensual. The sounds, smells and sensations of a crowd of humans is unlike anything I've ever experienced. Before my accident and the resulting phobia of going off-planet, I'd been to a dozen different systems. I'd seen alien cultures where smelling someone is considered the highest of insults. Others where speaking directly to a stranger is forbidden. Another in which eye contact could earn you a stint in traveler's prison.

No matter what anybody else might say about our rudeness, our crassness, our incredibly lowbrow behavior, here on Earth, being around people is a cacophony of sensations. It's why we're the biggest tourist destination in three galaxies, even without the clean air, sandy beaches and resorts the other planets boast. Aliens come here to rub elbows, literally, with humans.

Just like I was doing now. For a moment the pedtread shuddered as somewhere along the line a crowd shifted. The vibration barely rocked any of us, just jiggled us enough so an arm nudged a back here, or a leg shifted against a thigh, there. I heard a dozen different snippets of conversation all around me. Someone was wearing rose perfume.

Roses. My fingers clutched convulsively on my bag, where I'd stashed the florb. Declan had sent me roses.

"Excuse me." I moved around the man standing next to me and jumped off the pedtread.

In the second it took my feet to adjust to a nonmoving floor, I cursed under my breath. A couple passing me on the platform gave me an odd look, but I just flashed my tatbadge at them and they continued on without a backward glance. I've never really gotten used to how Ops are easily the most visible and overlooked people around.

I'd disembarked a good four blocks from the spa. I looked back to the pedtread trundling past me, and its cargo of passengers, and decided I'd walk. The exercise would be good for me, and I wouldn't risk any more unexpected thoughts of...him.

I sidestepped the hovertaxi waiting at the curb and headed for the raised catwalk above the street. My boots clanged on the metal stairs as I climbed. The walk was only about four meters above the street, but the extra height allowed a wafting breeze to hit my face as I walked.

Below me, traffic puttered without cease and the murmur of voices from the pedtread ebbed and flowed as it moved closer or further from my metal path. I was the only one up here. For one moment, I paused with my hands on the railing, my eyes closed, imagining the ocean.

But only for a moment.

When I finally reached the spa, my uniform already clung to my skin with sweat. Twenty years ago, when the city put up the anti-UV dome to keep out the cancer causing solar rays, someone had screwed up the ventilation system. Consequently, we live in a humid, sticky artificial atmosphere. It beats waking up with melanoma, though.

The retscan flashed in my eyes and the door opened for me. I entered another world. Air scented to smell like nothing but air greeted my nose. The temperature and humidity dropped. Only the hushed noise of slippered feet traversing the plush artigrass floor met my ears. This spa, The Mental Break, prided itself on offering its clientele something they lacked in the outside world. Peace. Serenity. A few minutes to unwind before they started punishing their bodies on the exercise machines or in the workout rooms.

"Hello, Miss Gemma." Jake, the door attendant, took my uniform as I slid out of it, then waited for my boots. "Nice to see you again."

Jake is an asex, having voluntarily undergone the operation after puberty's hormones had settled down. It was a little unsettling to watch his eyes slide over me without his dick even twitching in response, but refreshing, too. Sex is my business, even when it's a pleasure. It's nice to get a break from it sometimes.

I paid extra to belong to A Mental Break because of Jake, and because the spa allowed its members to compete physically instead of having only comgen programs. Today, I really needed to get some hand to hand. Work my body in a way that wasn't sexual. Get my mind off Declan.

"Hey, Gemma!" The petite brunette standing by one of the workout rooms waved.

"Britney. Ready for me to kick your butt?"

She laughed. "As if."

Britney is a rethead, completely into retro. Her era of choice is the 20's. Boy bands, patriotism, low-rise jeans, the works. She'd even changed her name in honor of the decade's hottest pop princess, Britney Spears.

Once inside the room, she stopped laughing. Without even waiting for me to get settled, she launched herself at my back. I bent low, and she flipped over. She hit the padded floor with an "oof!"

"Ouch." I didn't offer her a hand up. "That looks like it's got to hurt."

"I'm just getting warmed up." Britney leaped to her feet in a move that always astounded me, then faced off with her hands in a birdlike pose. "I'm going to get totally Neo on your ass."

"How many times have you seen that movie, anyway?" I matched her pose, one leg lifted, ready as if to fly.

"Last count? Five hundred."

"Still go to the midnight showings?"

She shook her head. "Nah. I ripped my Trinity vinyl pants. I'll get a new pair Offworld next week."

"Don't you ever stay home for more than two weeks at a time?"

"Are you kidding?"

She didn't ask me to go with her, because Britney knew better. I gave her the move she loved to give me before she had the chance to, a little wiggle of the fingers the movie hero made before pounding its villain. "Bring it on, shorty!"

Aided by the room's lowgrav function, we met in the air like eagles. Her foot connected squarely with my midsection. Now it was my turn to hit the floor with a thud. Britney didn't show mercy; she kneed me in the place my kidneys had been. Since they'd been replaced with replaceable, flexible mesh filters, the blow didn't hurt me as much as it might have someone without my enhancements.

"Not fair!" She bounced a little on the padded floor. "You're

28

enhanced. How'm I supposed to beat that?"

"You're not."

We fought each other, hard, until the timer signaled our turn in the room had ended. The room smelled of clean, exhausted sweat. Britney had thoroughly kicked my butt. Already bruises purpled several spots on my body.

"What's with you today?" She asked as we headed for the spa's after workout bliss area. "I've never been able to beat you this bad. You were way distracted, dude."

"I'm not a dude, Britney."

"What-eveh." She waved her hand. "Are you okay?"

"I need a massage and a soak in the hot tub. Then I'll be fine." I hoped I was right. While I'd been able to forget about the florb, and Declan, while Britney and I had been sparring, now that my body was unoccupied my mind started to wander again.

We picked tables side by side and punched in the keycodes for what we wanted. In seconds the massagebots whirred out of their slots in the floor and proceeded to pummel, knead and pound away our aches and pains. There was no way to mistake the sensation of wheels and rubber mallets for human fingers, and I breathed a silent sigh of relief. It wouldn't remind me of...him.

"Who is he?"

Britney's question startled me so suddenly I jerked on the table, and the bot let out a shrill warning beep.

"Remain still, please."

She repeated the question.

"I don't know what you mean."

"Shut UP! You do too. I've never seen you act this way before, Gemma. It has to be a guy. It's not Steve, is it? He hasn't...?"

"No." I sighed. "Steve hasn't done anything."

"Thank God-of-choice. I thought maybe he was coming after you for support again."

After my repairs had made me eligible to become an Op, Steve had believed he was entitled a share of my earnings. He'd lost the case. That the man I'd loved and agreed to spend my life with had reduced that love to a credit amount still burned, but not like it used to. Time heals all wounds, I guess.

"No."

"So, spill it!" Britney wiggled on the table while the bot worked on her back. "You're dating again!"

"Not exactly."

I heard the frown in her voice. "What does that mean?"

"I pulled in a PSSN-M last night for a routine check. Took him back to the inspection station, put him through his paces...."

"And?"

"And he made me come."

She paused before answering. For a long moment all I heard was the thumping of rubber wheels against flesh. "Good for you!"

"He wasn't a bot, Britney. I made a mistake."

"Damn, girl!"

I let the massagebot roll me over to work on my front. "I've never done that before. Misidentified."

"Why did he do it?" Britney sounded as mystified as I felt. "Doesn't he know that's illegal? I mean, asking you out is one thing, but fucking you in an inspection station!"

"He said he had a thing for the XTC 90."

"So he misidentified you, too." Britney's massagebot barked out a metal-toned "thank-you," and slid back into its slot. Mine did the same a moment later.

I sat up on the table, my skin still sheened with oil. "It's an easier mistake to make then the one I made."

"Don't be so hard on yourself. It does happen, doesn't it?" Britney hopped off the table and waited while I did the same.

"Not to me."

She gave me a thoughtful look as we headed for the hot tub. I punched the refill button that spurted steaming water into the two-person sized unit. I didn't ask her what she was thinking. I knew Britney well enough to guess.

"Are you going to see him again?"

"Not if I can help it."

We settled into the water with mutual sighs and let the jets pound against us.

"Why not? He made you come!" Britney leaned forward, getting in my face. "When's the last time that happened with a real person, not some holo program?"

I shook my head. "That doesn't matter, Britney."

"How long?"

"Since Eddie." I sighed and let myself float, eyes closed. "A long time ago."

I felt her hand on my arm. "You should see him again. Off-duty."

"He thinks I'm a metalgirl." I thought of the way his eyes had burned into mine just before he left. "He's not into mecho."

"You don't know that."

I opened my eyes and spoke harshly enough to make her flinch. "Most people aren't into mecho."

She put her hand on my shoulder. "Don't let what Steve did to you turn you off forever, Gemma."

Then she left me alone in the steaming water.

*   *   *

See him again. How could I do that? We'd committed a crime together, however unintentionally. I'd exacerbated the situation by not reporting it. My reason for dishonesty still bothered me. I hadn't wanted him to get into trouble.

I wasn't so afraid of reconditioning. It meant a training period, a loss of some privileges, perhaps some pay docking. But I wouldn't serve time. As Britney had said, it happens.

Declan, on the other hand, would face more serious charges. I'd told him they were harder on civilians because Ops are supposed to know better, but the fact is, any man or woman approached as a Pleasurebot by an Op is supposed to reveal their humanity. Instantly. No clever banter, no sidestepping the facts. Since it was easy enough to prove, they had no excuse for not doing it.

Unless, like Declan, they enjoyed walking the dangerous line. Anger suddenly rushed through my veins. Who the hell did he think he was? Because he got his rocks off fucking metalgirls, he'd jeopardized my job?

I must have made some angry noise, because the man standing next to me on the pedtread gave me a glance and moved away. By the time I got back to my apartment, I'd worked myself into a near rage. I walked so fast up to the door the retscan almost didn't have time to register me. I kicked the bottom of the door before it had a chance to open, and let out a string of curses.

"Is something wrong with my Gemma?" My fairy, Kaelyn, fluttered her wings and clasped her hands together. "Can Kaelyn do anything for her Gemma?"

As it usually did, the sight of the pretty creature calmed me. I stroked a length of her long, pale hair. "No, Kaelyn."

"Food for my Gemma? Drink?" She turned toward the kitchen, and her light gown seemed to float. "I've prepared dinner for my Gemma."

My desire to rage at the world for Declan's stupidity slowly drained away. Kaelyn smiled and went to the hook where she kept my robe. Without asking, she held it up for me.

"Thank you, Kaelyn."

The smooth material felt heavenly against my skin. Kaelyn took my crumpled and stained uniform and disappeared with it into the bedroom. Before I had time to make it to the kitchen, she was back.

"Sit," she cooed in her musical voice. It reminded me of wind chimes. "I will bring my Gemma something to drink."

I hadn't bought her to be my slave, but that was the role Kaelyn had put herself in. I accepted it because to protest meant she'd dissolve into agonized tears. I couldn't handle the guilt.

She wasn't a real fairy, of course. Kaelyn was Keanican. I'd picked her up at an auction in District 23, one of the seedier parts of the city. She was half dead, bedraggled, nursing a broken wing. I'd paid way too much for her then, but every cent had proven worth it.

"Does my Gemma wish her feet rubbed?" Without waiting for an answer, Kaelyn handed me a glass of something hot and knelt at my feet. Her nimble fingers worked the tension in my toes and arches the bots at A Mental Break had missed.

I sipped the beverage experimentally. Kaelyn tried hard, but she was still little more than a child. This, however, was delicious. Minty and aromatic, with a hint of some foreign spice. I sipped again, and relaxed for the first time all day.

Keanicans are humanoid, though half human size. Their wings have no feathers, but instead are a complicated organ of bone, sinew and gauzy flesh. Something like a bat's wing, but prettier. Everything about them is fresh and pink and pretty, which is why the settlers who first colonized Keani called them fairies. They can't fly in Earth's denser gravity, though their graceful ways sometimes make them seem like they're floating. Even inside the anti-UV dome, which granted us .0001 percent lesser gravity, they can do little more than flutter their wings rapidly.

"My Gemma needs to sleep." Kaelyn finished rubbing my feet. "My Gemma did not sleep last night."

"No, I didn't." I chuckled at her reproachful glare. "I'll go to bed right after I eat."

The frown turned to a smile of such blazing beauty it vibrated in my heart. Keanicans give off nothing but love, all the time. Treat them with respect and they will shower you with affection in return. That was the reason I bought her. To love me when Steve no longer would.

"Kaelyn will bring the dinner, my Gemma."

She fluttered off to the kitchen and brought back a tray. The smells wafting from it were not as nice as the drink she'd given me. I poked at the plate with my spork. The gelatinous ruby red mass jiggled, then disintegrated.

"What is this?"

Kaelyn beamed at me proudly. "Blood pudding."

It couldn't be. Consumption of animal products hadn't been possible for at least 100 years. Not for anyone but the disgustingly wealthy, anyway. "What's it made from?"

"I had to make some substitutions, my Gemma."

I sighed, then tasted it. "Artiberry jelly?"

"My Gemma doesn't like it?"

My stomach rumbled. "I'm sure it will be delicious with some bread and artipeanut butter."

I ate the sandwich in the tiny kitchen while Kaelyn fluttered about me and chattered about her day. As I finished the last bite, Kaelyn spun around so fast her wings became a blur.

"Oh, my Gemma! I forgot! This came for you while you were away."

She went to the cabinet and pulled out a florb. My blood turned to ice as she handed the silver object to me. I let it drop to the table.

"What is it, my Gemma?" Kaelyn pressed her little hands to the florb. "I've never seen...ooh!"

She'd triggered the release, and a bouquet of roses, purple this time, sprouted in holo from the florb. A second later came the scent. He'd added another expensive option to the gift this time—a message.

The words formed themselves of shining gold letters that hovered an inch or so above the flower heads. TO MATCH YOUR HAIR.

I reached across and snapped it off. With a whirr, the florb closed. The scent, however, remained.

"My Gemma! What was that?"

I couldn't bear to send her tumbling into tears, so I didn't respond as harshly as I wanted. "It's called a florb. A flower orb."

She'd never seen one, because I'd never received one in the time she'd lived with me.

"Who sent it to my Gemma?"

"A man." I paused. "It's not important."

"I have never seen such flowers, my Gemma. This man must care for my Gemma very much." She touched the florb again, and her

33

musical laughter rang throughout the kitchen when the flowers bloomed again.

"I wouldn't say that." The bitterness must have crept into my tone, because she looked at me with wide eyes.

"My Gemma is angry?"

"Not at you, Kaelyn."

"At the flower man?" She cocked her head, then swooped around to look at the flowers from the other side. "But they are so lovely."

She was right. But I couldn't enjoy them. "You take them, Kaelyn."

She looked so stunned I wanted to cry. No matter how many nice things I did for her, she always acted so surprised. As though she weren't worthy of being loved as she loved me.

"I can't take my Gemma's flowers."

I handed her the silver ball. She sagged under its weight. Tears sparkled in her eyes, but she stopped to give me a kiss on the cheek before taking it away to her closet.

It was so easy to make her happy. I envied Kaelyn that ability. She'd been stolen from her home, abused, and sold like an object, not a person. Yet she always managed to find joy.

I cleaned my meager dinnerware and headed for my bedroom. I was suddenly, bone-achingly weary. My sleepless night and the workout with Britney were taking their toll.

The intercom buzzed just as I passed the door. I stopped like a thief caught with his hand in the safe. Nobody rang my buzzer. Nobody came to visit me. Ever.

"Who is it?" I had to clear my throat twice before I could speak, it had gone so dry.

A muffled answer came back, and my heart slowed. A wrong buzz. Someone trying to access the building, maybe, or….

BUZZZZ.

"Who is it?"

The voice was clearer this time, and I couldn't mistake the reply. It came over the intercom as clear as Kaelyn's laughter. The sound of it made me press my hands to my breastbone to keep my heart from jumping through my skin. He spoke only one word, but if he'd recited volumes it would have made no difference.

"Declan."

CHAPTER 4

As a newbie fresh from the R.I.O. Academy, I'd served a stint in Oldcity. Riots, looting, and constant violence. The works. I'd done my share of hard duty. I wasn't afraid of stuff like that, yet hearing Declan's voice through the speaker made my knees weak and my heart thud in my chest like a hammer.

I didn't want to answer. Didn't want to watch my hand reach toward the screen control, or see my fingers flip the switch that brought his face into view. Yet I did those things anyway, as if I had no control. No power against my body's longings.

His face swam into view, briefly distorted as he stepped too close to the camera. "Are you in there?"

I'd blocked the two way viewing, of course. Everyone did. How many times would we be caught, literally, with our pants down by unexpected visitors if we didn't? I could see him, but he couldn't see me.

"What do you want?"

If he was taken aback by my brusque reply, he didn't show it. "Did you get the flowers?"

I bit my lip until the taste of blood, extra bitter since I became mecho, flooded my tongue. "What do you want, Declan?"

My voice skipped on the syllables of his name. Like I was some crazy school kid or something, giggling over a first crush. I watched him look more closely at the camera, as though sheer desire could allow him to see me through its lens.

"I want you. To see you."

"Go away."

My finger reached for the button that would disconnect us, but his voice stopped me. "Gemma, wait!"

I didn't want to wait any more than I'd wanted to answer his call in the first place. Yet I did. I cursed silently, but I did as he asked.

"Will you come down?"

I shook my head before remembering I had blocked the two way screening. "No."

He looked into the camera lens, and gave no trace of a smile. I could have stood against him if he'd made a joke, or tried to act seductive. His seriousness wooed me more than silly pretenses would have.

"Please," Declan said, and my resolve broke as easily as my bones had when my hoverscooter crashed into the side of the mountain.

"Give me a minute."

I clicked off the viewscreen and turned to the bedroom. Kaelyn, probably curious about the caller, had crept from her closet to watch me with wide eyes.

"Is that my Gemma's flower man?"

"Yes, Kaelyn." I brushed past her and into my bedroom.

The fairy followed me, her wings aflutter and her hands rubbing nervously together. "Is my Gemma going out?"

I nodded and went to my closet. "I have nothing to wear."

Kaelyn tilted her head, her expression confused. "My Gemma has lovely things to wear."

I rattled some of the hangers. "Nothing...pretty."

Kaelyn's wind chime laughter made me smile, at least. I couldn't stay sour in her presence. She went to the closet and riffled through the few garments I owned which were not uniforms or workout clothes.

"This." She pulled out an outdated gown I'd worn to go to a party for Steve's parents. "This will look pretty on my Gemma."

I caught sight of my reflection in the full length mirror on back of the door. The sight made me sink to the bed. I stared, hard, at the fine silver scars which were the only physical sign of my accident. Perhaps only I could really see them. But I could never forget them.

"Forget it." My harsh words made Kaelyn's big blue eyes well up with tears. "I don't need to look pretty."

Shrugging away her offers to fix my hair, I slipped into a dark gray jumpsuit. It wasn't a uniform. My uniforms are sexier.

36

I twisted my hair on top of my head. My cosmetics had been refreshed last week, so my face was fine. All I had to do now was go downstairs and meet him.

He wasn't waiting for me when I got off the lift. As disappointment I tried to deny pierced me, the scent of roses drifted to my nose. I turned. He'd been waiting for me.

"I brought you these." He held out another florb. "In case you didn't get the other two."

Now came the cocky smile I remembered. My anger returned, and I moved without thinking. My fist connected with his jaw hard enough to make him stagger back, even though at the last minute I pulled the force of my blow so I only hurt him, not killed him.

He managed to keep his feet, and incredibly, came up smiling. "I guess I deserved that."

I turned on my heel to make it back to the lift, but he reached out and managed to snag my elbow.

"Gemma. Don't."

I stopped, stiff as if I had iron beneath my skin instead of flexible copper/aluminum alloy. "Get your hands off me, Declan."

"I came here to apologize."

The lobby of my building is never empty. Today was no exception. I watched from the corner of my eye as an elderly couple who lived a few floors below me got on the lift. They didn't need to witness this. I heard their appalled whispers, and the word "mecho," and didn't need to hear more.

Without talking to him I stalked across the sterile marble floor and through the doors. The street outside hummed with activity. I heard the doors whisk open behind me, and sensed his presence at my back.

"What do you want?" I met his gaze as though looking into his eyes didn't send shivers of anticipation down the wires making up the bulk of my spinal cord.

"I told you. I came to apologize." Again, he held out the florb. When he pushed the button on this one, green roses bloomed in front of me.

I spoke before the gadget had time to project its golden-lettered messaged. "Put that away."

To my surprise, he did. Then he looked at me. Hard, for a few moments that felt like an eternity. I lifted my chin and held my stance. I'm usually good about keeping my emotions hidden. Usually it doesn't really matter. In front of him, it did. I'd be damned before I let him see how he affected me.

"Did you get in trouble at work?" His question hung in the humid air between us.

I didn't want to talk on the street in front of my building. I started walking. Declan followed. He didn't speak again until we both reached the gate of a public garden two buildings away from mine. As a resident of this District, my fully paid fee and my retscan would automatically open the doors, but I paused with my eyes averted before the scan could catch my gaze.

"I didn't get in trouble." Then I turned my head, the gates opened, and we went inside.

*   *   *

The grass and trees inside were real. So were the flowers, stunted and cheerless though they might be. The dome which kept us all from disintegrating into cancerous lumps also made it hard for the plants to grow.

A fountain, also real instead of holo, forced a fine spray of water into the air at precisely timed intervals. The water wasn't real. It wouldn't even wet your fingers if you touched it, though its chemical components contained hydrogen and oxygen, and it was potable if you were desperate.

Declan followed me down the gravel path, wisely not saying anything. When we got to a plazglass bench carved to look like stone, I sat. After a moment, he sat too.

"I didn't get in trouble because I didn't give an honest report," I said without preamble. I looked him in the eye. "I would have been reprimanded if I'd filled out the IIP paperwork. Possibly suspended, since R.I.O. is really cracking down on offenses like this. But you—"

Declan nodded. "I'd have been arrested."

"You knew the penalties. But you went with me anyway. Why?" The muted sun cast his dark hair with threads of auburn and gold. Real highlights, not cosmetics. Glory, this man was beautiful.

"I told you why." He set the florb on the bench between us.

I gave a short laugh. "Yeah. You have a 'thing' for the XTC 90."

I expected the slanting, mocking grin, but again he surprised me by remaining straight faced. "Yes, I do."

I got up from the bench and the gravel crunched beneath my feet. "There are plenty of freeboots out there, Declan. You don't have to break the law to get off."

He quirked a brow at me. "I know you're not a bot. I didn't at first, but I figured it out pretty quick."

"But you said—"

"I know what I said," Declan interrupted. "Hey, you thought I was a PSSN. I thought you were an XTC 90. I think we both know when we realized the truth."

So he didn't think I was a bot. He wasn't interested in just a fling with a metalgirl, but something with a fleshgirl. Me. But he didn't know I am mecho, and that made a world of difference.

The anger masking my insecurity was real, however. He'd taken an incredible risk, not just for himself, but for both of us.

I clenched my fists. "Don't you get it? They're arresting people for this! And they're not getting slaps on the wrist, either. I could get suspended, but you could go to work camp!"

Unconsciously, I'd widened my stance and rested my left hand on my belt, close to my stunner. When I realized I was going into battle mode, though, I didn't change it.

Declan's gaze took in my body language. The slight smile and the way he briefly opened and closed his hands told me he knew I was itching for a fight—and that he didn't care.

"Most people try to avoid the work camps." My voice didn't tremble, through sheer force of will.

"Why should you care if I get sent to a work camp?" He took a step closer to me. "That's your reason for not filing the report? You were trying to save me?"

Pride prevented me from stepping back. "I don't want to get suspended, either."

Another step. I could feel the warmth of his breath stir the tendrils of my hair. "But I'm sure not filing the right report would get you more than just suspension. It could get you fired or demoted. Right?"

He crushed his mouth down on mine. I reacted instantly by bringing up my arms to push him away. With a shocking strength, he pinned my arms to my sides. He might be bigger, might even be as strong, but I was still quick. I hooked a leg in back of his knee and we hit the ground hard enough to send drops of synthwater spraying from the fountain.

Bright blood blossomed on his mouth where my teeth had caught his lips. He still had my arms pinned, but now my weight rested on him. My thigh pressed firmly between his legs, ready to jerk upward if I thought I needed the advantage.

Against my belly, the thickness of his erection nudged me. He blinked and ran his tongue across his mouth. The blood smeared. He smiled.

"I haven't been able to stop thinking about you since last night."

"Shut up."

Any normal opponent would have been no match for me. Yet in Declan's grip I might as well have been unenhanced. He pressed me closer to him, his grip on my wrists hard enough to bruise. He rocked his hips upward, just enough for me to feel the way his penis bulged beneath his pants.

"I've been hard all day, thinking about it."

"Let me go."

He pulled me another inch closer. "Tell me you haven't been thinking about me, and I will."

He let go of my wrists and put his hands on my hips. The warmth of his fingers caressed me through the thin material of my jumpsuit. His thigh between my legs came up to press against my center, once, twice, hard enough to turn me on. The electric tingle shot through me.

"Your eyes just got darker," he said. "Don't tell me you don't want me as bad as I want you."

The press of the gravel against my knees forced some sense into my sex-befuddled mind. I forced myself off him and to my feet.

"What we did was a crime that could get us both into a lot of trouble. I don't like trouble."

He had the swiftness and grace of some sort of feline, like the sabrecats in the zoo. Declan got to his feet. "Tell me."

I shook my head. "Damn you."

"You can't, can you? You've been thinking about me, haven't you? All day long?"

I turned to face the fountain. My fingers clenched, hard, against my palms. Hard enough to cut. My reply ground its way like shards of glass from my throat.

"Damn you. Yes."

He put his hands on my shoulders, then slid the fingers down my arms. His lips found the exposed flesh of my neck. I felt the hot swipe of his tongue along the downy edges of my upswept hair, and my knees nearly buckled. His touch hit me in my breasts, my clit, the pit of my stomach.

The artificial water splashed and chimed against the fountain's plazglass basin. I gave myself to Declan without words, a silent assent he nevertheless understood perfectly. I reached one hand up and back to caress his hair and press his mouth harder to the back of my neck.

His hands found the fullness of my breasts and cupped them. He pinched my nipples through my jumpsuit; I moaned. He slid his hands down my sides, over my hips, and finally to where I needed them most. I sagged against him when he pressed the fingers of his right hand to my mound.

"Tell me you thought about me doing this to you," he whispered in my ear.

"I thought of this. Of you."

"Tell me you want me, now."

I told him, hating myself for giving in so easily but finding a kind of relief in it, too. This was my fantasy, my holo program. A lover who didn't fear my strength. One who knew just how to touch me, to stroke me. One who could make me come.

"I want to taste you."

His simple words caught me on fire. With another moan, I arched against him. He turned me and with gentle pressure urged me to rest my backside against the fountain's plazglass base.

Color stood high on his tawny cheeks, and his broad chest rose and fell with his rapid breathing. The sight of his arousal made my own breath come faster. Before I had time to really admire him, Declan knelt in the grass at my feet. I braced my hands on the fountain's rim, and watched him. He found the snaps at the jumpsuit's crotch and tugged them open.

The air in the enclosed garden wasn't cool, but it felt like ice compared to my sex-heated flesh. I shivered. He smiled.

Declan dipped his head between my thighs and kissed my sexbutton. It throbbed. He spread me with his fingers, softly, and his tongue darted against me with a series of flickering movements so light I could barely feel them.

This was insane. I knew it. Anyone in the res-dist could walk in here, any time. It was insane…but it wasn't illegal.

I gave myself up to the only man who'd taken me over the edge in five years. I couldn't help myself. I didn't want to. My body, which gave and received sex on a daily basis, craved something more than the thrustings and gropings of casual intercourse. It wanted something not even Nick and my customized holo could give me.

He slipped a finger inside me, and I opened for him. He slipped in two. His tongue worked the bundle of nerves while he slid his fingers in and out. It wasn't enough. It was too much. I was going to come again, and I wanted it. I wanted him.

He pulled away and slid up the length of my body. His thick penis stretched me, filled me. He bent his head to kiss my throat. His fingers gripped my shoulders.

"You feel so good," he whispered. "Gemma."

It was the way he said my name. Tender but rough at the same time, and filled with longing. He said my name like the taste of it pleased him.

I cried out, and buried my face in his shoulder to muffle the sound. My hands clutched his back. We rocked against the fountain, the spray of it hitting us but leaving us dry. His thrusts became ragged as he neared his climax, and I was right there with him.

I saw fireworks behind my closed eyes as the pleasure of my orgasm ripped through me. Red, blue, gold, the colors filled my vision until I opened my eyes and stared into Declan's face.

His gaze didn't waver from mine. He said my name again, lower this time, harsher, as though speaking had become some near impossible task. I shuddered as another orgasm rippled through me.

He never closed his eyes, not even when his own climax made him buck and shudder against me. He kept his gaze fixed on mine the entire time, and all the while he whispered my name.

It's funny how after orgasm the senses become so heightened. The garden's silence, unbroken but for the fountain's splashing, seemed as loud as a hovertrain when my heart's pounding faded from my ears. Declan rested his forehead briefly against mine. He could have kissed me had he tried, but I guess the split lip made him reconsider.

After-sex awkwardness isn't something I generally have to deal with. Pleasurebots don't care about conversation. They get off, they get you off, they consider themselves as having done their job.

People, on the other hand, insist on talking.

"Wait." I put a hand to his mouth when he started to speak. With the other, I pushed him gently off me. With efficient movements, I buttoned myself up again. The warmth of his seed coated me down there.

He tucked himself away, then ran a hand through his hair. "Are you all right?"

The simple consideration in his words made me pause. "I'm fine."

He frowned. "Just...fine?"

"What would you like me to say, Declan?"

Now his expression shuttered, his gaze clouded. "Something more than fine."

I'd been stupid to bring him here, and stupider to fuck him again. I pretended to fix my hair to disguise the sudden trembling of my fingers. I turned my head so I wouldn't have to see him.

"Okay, you got your jollies. Now you can go."

"Is that what you think?" His words had a thin edge of anger to them.

I needed to distance myself from him. There could be no future with Declan for me. The way we met and what I was precluded that.

"You got what you wanted from me. Now go."

"If you think that's all I wanted…" he paused, broke off, started again. "Gemma, I meant what I said when I haven't stopped thinking about you all day."

The sincerity in his tone wormed its way beneath the wall I was rapidly trying to build. "We shouldn't see each other. You know that. Not when it could mean…"

"You're not on duty now. We didn't do anything wrong."

"But last night I was on duty, and we committed a crime." I swallowed heavily. "Today can't change that."

"Last night is over." He gave me that damned cocky grin. "Today didn't bring it back. It's gone. I screwed up, made a mistake. But…I couldn't help myself."

"No?" I gave him a hard look. "You could have stopped the inspection at any time."

He ran a hand through his hair again. "I didn't want to. I told you…"

"Yeah, I know." My heart twisted. "You and your fetish for the XTC 90."

"I couldn't resist you, don't you get it?" He put his hands in his pockets and rocked on his heels. "No man could. And then today, I just wanted to see you again. Touch you again. Gemma, you might not believe this…"

"I'm sure I won't."

"But I haven't felt this way about anyone in a really long time." He took a deep breath. "In fact, before last night, I hadn't even slept with anyone in over a year."

This revelation stunned me into silence. It's unheard of for men and women past the age of sexual initiation to remain abstinent for such a length of time. Sex is indulged in as generously and casually as eating. It's the reason I have a job.

I didn't know what to say. "You must be joking."

He shook his head, then gave me just a ghost of a grin. "Not until I met you."

Our eyes met and our gazes locked. Who was this man? He had fooled me into thinking he was something he was not, he had made my body sing and my heart leap. Could I admit he had given me hope?

"I wasn't out at the 'hut last night looking to get laid," Declan said. "But then you swaggered up to me and flashed me your badge. Hell. I've been dreaming about the XTC 90 since my first wet dream. I couldn't refuse. Then when I realized you were a fleshgirl, it was even better."

"Declan." I rolled the name on my tongue like it was fine piece of chocolate. "I have to tell you. I'm—"

Then he reached out to tuck a strand of hair away behind my ear. The gesture, so simple, so insignificant, took my breath away. How long since someone had touched me like that? Without needing something from me? Without taking something from me? I was lost, and I knew it. Lost in a casual gesture from a man I barely knew.

"What, Gemma?"

I'd meant to tell him the truth. I'm not a metalgirl, and I'm not a fleshgirl. I'm mecho.

He cocked his head, waiting for me to speak, and I thought of how he'd whispered my name over and over. Like some sort of prayer. I thought of his lips pressed to mine, and I answered him.

"Nothing, Declan," I said. "It doesn't matter."

CHAPTER 5

We parted with the promise to meet again the next night.

"I'll come for you," he promised, and left the garden before I'd had the chance to ask him for his address or how I could reach him.

Mysterious. I laughed softly to myself as I let myself into the dark apartment. In Newcity, nobody truly has a private life—except for those who are wealthy enough to afford one. Everyone else's vital information is stored in System, and readily available at a retscan's notice. Everything from shoe size to favorite beverage can be found in those databanks. If I really wanted to find him, I could. For now, not knowing anything about him other than the taste of him was exciting.

I paused to peek in at Kaelyn, huddled in her closet. When I'd first brought her home, I'd made a bed for her in my room. I didn't know nights on Keani are perfectly, seamlessly black. It had taken several sleepless weeks before Kaelyn could explain to me why the faintest glow of light from the viddy screen's sleep setting made it impossible for her to sleep.

Even now, the faint glow let in when I opened the door made her stir. She blinked, slowly, and sighed.

"My Gemma."

"I'm home, Kaelyn. Go back to sleep."

With a drowsy nod, she snuggled back into the nest of blankets she preferred over a mattress, and went back to sleep. I paused a moment longer to stare at the strange creature I'd brought into my home. An impulse I didn't understand moved me to tuck the blankets around her more firmly, and to smooth the line of her folded wing as she dreamed. It wasn't my right to own her, this alien child, but I couldn't be sorry about it. She'd have died if I hadn't bought her and taken her to live with me. I was sure of that.

I closed the closet door and went to my hygiene room. I tossed my drab gray outfit into the recycling chute, then opened the small key panel next to my mirror and punched in the codes for a new set of clothes, some chocobars, and some other supplies for the next day.

System's smooth female voice reverberated in the small room. "Credit account charged. Items scheduled for delivery 05053005."

Naked, I looked myself over in the mirror above the sink. Even in the bright light, all but one of my scars were nearly invisible. The only one still obvious was the snaking line from the back of my neck across my throat and down my left shoulder. Even that had faded to a simple, silver line against the ivory of my skin.

Declan hadn't noticed the signs, and he'd have no other way of knowing for sure I am mecho, unless I told him. The thought did not appeal to me.

One day, I would be able to afford a real water shower. Until then, I had to settle for a regular artiwater shower. The synthetic H2O wrapped me in a shield of cleansing warmth when I stepped into the plazglass tube, but though it left me clean and refreshed, it lacked the sheer sensuality of natural water against the skin. I didn't even have to dry off.

I did have a real water bed, though, on which I still owed monthly payments. It was a luxury I had never regretted buying. I couldn't have imagined living without it.

Though I was still tired from my lack of sleep the previous night, the shower had refreshed me enough I couldn't go to sleep right away. Experience had also taught me that forcing myself to extend my sleep beyond the hour or so my body absolutely had to have to function normally usually ended up in me feeling less rested than if I only gave myself the 45 minutes. Being mecho had a lot of pluses and minuses, and I still couldn't decide which this was.

"Viddy on," I said as I lowered myself into the chair in my bedroom. "Something mindless."

"Command not recognized." System, for all it sounded like an attractive woman eager to complete your every command, was really just a computer program. Give her the right orders and you'd get what you want. Phrase something a little off, and forget it.

"Entertainment channel," I said. "Restrict pornography, restrict sports, restrict politics."

Apparently, that left only a chickvid fashion show. I had asked for something mindless. The show's hostess, Zilize Pesnnirf, was a vapid, ass-kissing socialite with a shrill laugh like the sound of brakes screeching. She specialized in interviewing prominent Newcitizens and Offworld celebs. Tonight's guest was Cyndira Adar, Howard Adar's wife.

"...truly tragic, some of them," Mrs. Adar was saying when the viddy screen locked onto the show. "And it really is amazing what they can do nowadays. But still, where do we draw the line?"

Zilize nodded, her thin lips pursed into a frown. "Oh, Cyn, I agree. Absolutely. I'm not against enhancement, understand—"

Cyndira let out a cultivated cackle. "Oh, heavens no! Enhancements are the best thing that's ever happened!"

Both women laughed together, their perfect coifs never moving. This sort of thing didn't interest me. I knew what they were going to say. The arguments in Newcity were growing more and more heated, what with the Newcity Ruling Council's latest push to legally classify mecho citizens as not human.

"But you have to draw the line somewhere," Cyndira continued, smoothing her face into lines of seriousness. She turned to look straight into the camera. "I mean, really, a more attractive profile and firmer body are one thing. We all appreciate beauty in all its forms, don't we? But when you talk about replacing actual organs and systems..."

She gave a delicate shudder, and Zilize picked up the conversation. "I completely agree, Cyndira. Looking good is one thing. Turning yourself into a bot is quite another!"

"Viddy off!" I barked the command, and had to take a deep breath to control my anger.

I didn't choose to become mecho, but if I had been given the chance to live or die, I'd have made the same choice. I could live without gargantuan breasts and a thin waist. I could even live without perfect vision and teeth. But without the organs and bones, sinews, veins and arteries the mechtechs in the hospital had given me, I wouldn't live at all.

"Where is the line?" I asked aloud to the dark viddy screen. "If it has to be drawn somewhere, where is it?"

"Inquiry not recognized," System replied. "Rephrase question."

"Forget it," I told the computer. "Inquiry retracted."

47

*   *   *

I woke the next morning groggy and out of sorts, until I remembered my plans for the evening. Declan had asked me for an evening in District 87, the arts District.

I didn't think anything could destroy my good mood, until I got into the office. The tension was palpable when I got there, and the silly grin I'd been wearing faded as my fellow Ops stared at me when I came in.

"What's going on?"

Lonnie jerked her chin toward the constantly scrolling viddy display on the far wall. "Ranking."

I clenched my jaw and took a look at the tiny letters and numbers making their slow way down the display. "Again?"

"It's not a big deal," put in Frude.

"Easy for you to say," Lonnie shot back. "You're not—"

The two Ops glanced at me, then fell silent. I forced a small smile to my face.

"It's okay," I told them. "I'm not sensitive."

"Orli is," muttered Frude. He looked over to the tall dark-haired Op watching the viddy display with folded arms and a scowling face.

"Orli's a kid," replied Lonnie. "This could mess up his future."

I wasn't flattered to no longer be considered young enough that a change in my Newcity rank couldn't affect my future, but I knew what Lonnie meant. Orli was fresh out of the R.I.O. Academy, with only a couple of months service under his belt. Any privilege and rank advancement he could hope to gain through his career had just been reduced. Not by much, but by enough. He'd have to work harder, and longer for the same benefit—and with the way things were going, even that might not help.

We had to stick together, us freaks. Though I didn't know Orli very well, I had helped with some of his rookie training. He was a bright kid, good looking, and smart. He had a lot going for him, and not just his innate sexuality that drew men, women and Pleasurebots to him like rats to a scrap of bread.

"Newcity Ruling Council." He spat the words like they tasted bad. He looked at me. "They just announced a shift in the ranks. I'm bumped down three whole slots."

I hadn't bothered to check my own rank, but I could assume the same treatment. "What's their reason this time?"

"They say," and he emphasized the word to show he didn't believe it, "that a group of techtechs have perfected the next System upgrade."

"How many of them?"

"Seven hundred and fifty." Orli punched one fist into the other. "Like that many techtechs ever work together on anything at once!"

"So now there's 750 Newcitizens who deserve a higher rank," I said. "Which means 750 others have been demoted."

"You want to know how many mechos are registered in Newcity?" Orli asked in a low voice filled with helpless anger. "Seven hundred and thirty-eight."

I clasped his shoulder. "A three-slip isn't anything to worry about, Orli. That won't even affect your ration count or your salary."

"Not until it becomes a ten-slip," he replied grimly. "I was going to marry Natalie this year."

"Don't let this change your plans," I told him. Envy flooded me, but only briefly. I refused to be jealous of this young man or the lovely young woman who'd agreed to bond with him.

The anger in his eyes shifted for one moment to bleakness. "She's getting a lot of pressure from her family. Her father's one of the undersecretaries for Ruling Council. He doesn't want her to marry me."

"That sucks donkey dicks, Orli."

My declaration seemed to startle him into a smile. "Yeah, big ones."

"Speaking of big ones," Lonnie broke in. "I hate to interrupt, but Captain Rando wants us all in the conference room."

"Hey, G," Eddie greeted as the Ops on duty filed into the conference room. "What's the happs?"

Despite the grim atmosphere, Eddie couldn't fail to bring a grin back to my face. Now was not the time or place to tell him about my recent activities, so I just said nothing.

Eddie didn't have time to ask me anything else, either, because Rando entered the conference room. Her hoverchair turned effortlessly on its cushion of air as she took her place at the front of the room.

Seeing Rando out from behind her desk was still worth a second glance, even after my many years with R.I.O. Her legs had been withered by an Offworld disease contracted during her service in the Earthen/Livannone War fifteen years ago. She'd opted for a hoverchair, increased rank and a desk job instead of cosmetic enhancement and repair. It was so unusual to see someone with flaws of such a grand nature, that even after all this time we all paused for a moment as she took her place in the front of the room.

"By now, you'll all have heard," she announced. Her plazglass lenses reflected the shimmering light of the viddy display still scrolling behind us. "This news affects the entire department. The physical requirements of employment with any of the Special Ops departments, including Recreational Intercourse, means it's a natural choice for those citizens who've found themselves through choice or chance enhanced."

She glanced down at her legs, thin and twisted inside the navy artisilk uniform she wore. "For some, it's more chance than choice. But for whatever reason, you all know we have a higher percentage of mecho employees than in any other department or trade guild in Newcity. Until the past year or so, that worked in our favor. Since the Ruling Council started its latest campaign, I'm ashamed to say that is no longer true."

"You mean since Howard Adar started accusing mechos of not being human, you mean." Orli's strong voice echoed through the room.

I envied him his confidence, but shook my head a little at his brashness. I can kick ass from here to next year if I have to, but only if I have to. Spouting my mouth about things I can't change has never been my method. It causes trouble, and I've had enough of that.

"When more than 50 percent of your body has been replaced with metal and fiber," put in Frude, "what can you expect?"

There might have been a fight, but for Rando's sharp snort. Nobody wanted to mess with her. She didn't need her legs to kick anybody's ass.

Orli backed down, glowering. Frude just shrugged and gave the rest of the assembled Ops an innocent look. Frude's attitude hadn't earned him many friends in R.I.O—but it hadn't exactly made him any enemies, either.

"Times are changing," Rando continued. "Maybe not for the better. But we're here to do a job the best we can. I will not let common bias and prejudice come between any members of this team, am I clear?"

"And when they take away our citizenship?" Orli asked, giving it one last try. "What then, Cap'n?"

Rando met his gaze without flinching. "Let's hope that doesn't happen, Orli."

He didn't say anything else. I felt the weight of a dozen pairs of eyes on me, but if I looked around I couldn't seem to get anyone to meet my gaze. I'd never made a secret of my condition to anyone...except Declan.

Rando continued. "Along with the recent ranking changes, the Ruling Council has also implemented some new regs for the entire

SpecOps department, including R.I.O."

A low groan rippled through the group. New regs meant training time, at three quarters pay.

"Obviously, we can't have all Ops tied up in training. Pleasurebot related incidents have risen .003% since last year. So half of you will hit the field while the rest participate in the new training. Then we'll switch."

Eddie nudged me. "I caught a glimpse of the new protocols. Hot stuff."

I rolled my eyes. Rando was reading off the list of partners. "So some manufacturer puts out a new set of specs on its models, and we have to be updated. When you come right down to it, even the Kama Sutra only has so many positions."

"You're awfully young to be so jaded," Eddie told me, which was a laugh since he's exactly my age.

"EDDE 08111977, GMMA 03271971."

"That's us, surprise." I gave him a wink. "Let me go beat your butt."

Eddie grinned. "I look forward to it."

It turned out the new regs were for the HTTIE 750, the latest Pleasurebot to hit the stores. It was the most expensive bot on the market, and most were still privately owned. A few used models had started to trickle into the pricier Lovehuts now, and several problems had been detected. Nothing quite as serious as the PSSN's malfunctioning ignition, but the sexbot industry couldn't afford any bad publicity.

"Not much like the GRLFRND 220, huh?" Eddie remarked as we entered the training room.

The Girlfriend model had been the most popular in history—until it became obvious that once the warranty expired, the bot's ditzy nature turned to maudlin self-pity. Privately owned models were the worst— sold into service or even those given up to work as freebots, the Girlfriends became suicidal at being sent away from the men and women who'd bought them originally. Expired-warranty Girlfriends had taken to self annihilation all over the place, sometimes taking their unfortunate clients with them. It had been the biggest scandal in Pleasurebot history, but had reaffirmed to all Newcitizens the importance of R.I.O. Interestingly, the equivalent male model, the BYFRND 220, hadn't had any problems at all. What that said about the differences inherent between men and women, I couldn't tell you.

"I'm a Hottie Model." The bot flipped her cascade of blonde hair over one perfect shoulder and looked down her nose at me. "Not a Girlfriend. I'm the most advanced and expensive model out there."

"I see the snob function works perfectly," I remarked, not bothered by her dismissal of me.

"Some men prefer an aloof partner," said the Hottie. "It validates their belief that they're escorting the finest Pleasurebot available."

"In other words," Eddie said, "Some guys like getting it on with chicks who'd would turn them down if they were flesh."

The Hottie sniffed. "I've had two owners, both of who were ecstatic with my performance."

"Not ecstatic enough to keep you very long," I mentioned. She didn't respond. She probably wasn't programmed to react to criticism. I glanced at her specsheet. "And now you're a freebot, registered in District 56?"

"Yes."

"Available for private jobs through appointments at the following: Xtasy, Xanadu and Perfect Partner?" I named three of the most prominent kennels in that District.

She gave a supercilious smirk. "That's right."

Eddie took a peek at the specsheet. "Says here you've had several complaints about being difficult to stimulate."

Her pretty features creased momentarily. "I undergo daily diagnostics. I perform perfectly."

I looked over our instructions, which included a log of complaints. The instructions included a list of malfunctions, most of them minor, and the specific workarounds to eliminate them. I'd never take in a bot for something as stupid as this, but if the order came down from above, it had to have been backed by the manufacturer. The companies don't want to lose business.

"Eddie, this looks right up your alley."

She allowed herself to look curious. "What's it say?"

"Says here we're supposed to stimulate you to climax three times."

She shifted in her chair, crossing one long, perfect leg over the other. The artisilk skirt clung to her thighs like a second skin. "No problem."

"In under an hour."

She still didn't look concerned, even though her diagnostic report clearly showed an inadequately tuned climax dial. She must have been programmed with a healthy dose of attitude.

"Let's get started." I unsnapped my jumpsuit and hung it up on the wall hook. I checked my internal clock. "I need to get out of here on time tonight."

*   *   *

I'm not a HTTIE 750, but I had to admit I looked pretty good. The personal holo image from which I'd selected the dress had shown it would flatter my figure. In reality, it did more than simply make me look pretty. It made me feel pretty.

It wasn't in style, not with the long sleeves and high neckline. Current Newcity fashion ran to sheer fabrics and exposed skin. Only the back opened low to the first swell of my buttocks. The color was a deep, rich plum that softened the violet hue of my hair and emphasized the natural blue of my eyes. I wore a thin pair of slippers with it, and my feet felt so light after removing my standard footwear I almost thought I could fly.

I forced myself not to shift as I waited outside the restaurant. Emily's is the hottest eatery in District 87. I'd never been there...but since I hated eating in restaurants alone, I hadn't been much of anywhere in eight years.

Declan was late, and I tried not to let that bother me. I filled my time watching the outdoor viddy screen. Its visual had split, with the city ranking still scrolling on the left and a Donball tournament showing on the right.

Nobody waiting to get in tonight had to worry about their Newcitizen rank. The cream of Newcity society mingled outside the doors of Emily's. I recognized several faces from the viddy screen. Nobody really famous, nobody really powerful. B-list celebs, at most. Still, it was interesting to note that Frank Phillips' hair was grayer in real life than on viddy, and his wife fatter.

There were more reports from the Ruling Council about citizen classification protocols.

"Nobody's saying that bots should be given citizenship," one talking head was saying. "That's ridiculous. Bots are made, not born."

"Are you denying the rights of artificial womb babies?" A woman on the screen yelled out.

"That's different," put in another debater. "They're human, no matter how they were conceived. Bots are made of metal and wire. They have computer chips for brains."

"And what about mechos, then?" Cried another woman. "Once the body's dead, shouldn't it stay that way?"

I turned from the screen, disturbed. I thought I heard a couple of muttering whispers, but shrugged them off. The bottom line is, unless you know for sure about me, you just can't tell. The medtechs had done an excellent job in that respect.

I ignored the sinking in my gut when fifteen minutes passed, then fifteen more. I checked my internal clock against the numbers on top of the viddy screen and was disappointed to find they were the same.

The crowd thinned as the dinner hour, even for the fashionably late, passed. My stomach growled. I waited another ten minutes, then turned on my heel and headed for the pedtread.

A green-uniformed courier stopped me just before I got on. "GMMA 03271971?"

"Yes."

"I have a delivery for you." He flashed a portable retscan in my eyes to confirm identity, then handed me the lightweight silver box. As he rode away, I thumbed the button on top of the box to activate the holomessage inside.

GEMMA

The letters formed in a golden haze an inch above the box.

RAN INTO SOME PROBLEMS. WILL NOT BE ABLE TO GET TO EMILY'S. I'M WAITING AT CHEZ GARNER.

*D

"Screw that," I muttered and tossed the holocube into the closest incinerator. "I waited 45 minutes for him. I'm not that much of a sap."

But I was. When the next courier caught me on the next block and gave me a florb, which opened to reveal a spray of daisies and ferns, I changed my mind about meeting Declan. I didn't like myself for doing it, because it went against my nature to cater to a man like that. I'll admit the thought of not seeing him broke my pride better than anything else could have—except the second holocube and its one word message.

PLEASE.

*   *   *

Chez Garner isn't quite as high-class as Emily's, but the food is good and the company delightful. In truth, I doubt I could recall now what I even ordered, only that the meal was warm and the beverages cold.

We talked a lot, sparring our words back and forth across a checked tablecloth. The waitrons had begun to dim the lights and make rude noises about the time when we left. Declan linked his hand through

54

mine as we went through the doors.

We revealed everything and nothing about ourselves. Our secret dreams, our favorite foods, the names of our first sexual partners. We spoke of nothing that hadn't happened within the last year or less than ten years before. If Declan noticed the glaring gap in my recounted history, he said nothing. I did the same for him.

We walked, hands linked, along metal catwalks and looked down at the traffic below. We stared up at the night sky, tinged with a plethora of colors from Newcity's thousands of neon signs. We talked about stars, though we could see none. We just...talked.

Declan had a lazy, crazy sense of humor that had me chuckling at the least provocation.

"When's the last time you laughed like this?" He asked me, when I had to take my hand from his to wipe a tear from my eye. He'd pointed out how the trendsetters all looked the same from above, and likened them to a species of Lebanonian bird that displays its feathers to attract a mate, but ultimately is sexually impotent.

I thought. "It's been a long time."

He took my hand back again, and pressed it to his mouth. My laughter cut off with a small gasp at the sensation of his tongue flicking once, twice, against my palm. He closed my fingers around the kiss and gave me a look I couldn't mistake.

"We need to go somewhere," he said.

I nodded, but thought of Kaelyn, asleep by now in her closet. "Not my place."

"Not either of our places," he replied. "I have a better idea."

The Laughing Woman wasn't a Lovehut I was familiar with, though I'd heard of it. I glanced dubiously at the sign, which featured an obese women, hands on her knees, laughing. Her neon lips opened, closed, opened, closed, in silent hysterics.

Inside, however, the hut was tastefully decorated and nearly empty. Declan waved me down a hallway and opened one of the doors. The room inside surprised me as well. It was clean, and smelled sweet, and the only indication this was a room made solely for sex was the enormous bed that was the only furniture.

It will sound crazy, but suddenly I was as shy as a newbie. Heat bloomed in my cheeks, and I shook it off. We'd already been together, yet the evening we'd spent together had changed things in a subtle way.

"Very nice." I touched the bed. Soft. I looked at Declan, who'd ceased his joking and now only looked at me with a serious glint in his chocolate colored eyes.

"I wanted it to be nice."

I cleared my throat and looked from him to the bed. "Declan."

He tilted his head. "Yes, Gemma."

"Come here." I crooked my finger at him.

"Always have to be in charge, don't you?" He asked, but there was no sting in his words. He took me in his arms. I had to tilt my head to return his kiss, and the tickle of my hair on my bare back made me feel dreamy and disconnected. Our mouths opened, our tongues danced. His hands on my skin made me realize I was naked, and I hadn't noticed when my dress fell into puddle on the floor.

With no sense of urgency, I unbuttoned his shirt while we kissed and his hands roamed my skin. I slipped the thin material off his shoulders, down his arms, past his hands, and laid him bare for my appreciation.

"I'm glad you came to Chez Garner," Declan said. "I wasn't sure you would."

"I almost didn't." I traced the outline of his nipples with my fingertips and enjoyed the way his skin prickled into goose bumps. His skin was smooth, and nearly hairless but for the twin circles on his chest and the line disappearing into his trousers.

I paused to lightly touch the pale spot of a scar on his throat. "What happened?"

He took my hand from the spot and put it back on his chest. "Hoverbike accident."

I didn't ask again. I didn't want to remember my own scars, my own accident. Instead, I concentrated on dipping my head to tongue his salty flesh. He didn't wear a belt, and his dark pants were made in the current fashion of no snaps, buttons or zippers. I loosened the drawstring and let the material open wide enough to slide over his hips. Again, he wore black briefs that accentuated the bulge of his erection.

I slid my hands to his hips and tilted my forehead to rest against his chest. Declan put his arms around me, lightly, not pressing. It occurred to me with a sudden shiver that I was just as happy to stand like that with him as I was to be having intercourse.

"Cold?" He wrapped his arms around me more firmly.

The simple gesture made feelings I wasn't sure I wanted to feel rocket through me. I didn't have time to pursue them, though, because he put a finger beneath my chin so I had to stare into his eyes. We said nothing, but the silence wasn't awkward. It was charged with expectation.

I hooked my thumbs in his waistband and slid the briefs down, and followed the motion by sinking onto my knees before him. I've said before going down on a man gives me a sense of power, but I didn't feel that with Declan then. It seemed at that moment this wasn't about power, or advantage. I took the length of him in my mouth because, right then, I wanted to please him more than I wanted any other thing.

He groaned a little and pushed himself deeper into my mouth. The scent of him, soap, clean clothes, arousal, filled my nostrils and made my thighs jump in expectation. I stroked my hands down his legs and cupped my hands around his calves. The crinkly hair brushed my knuckles. The muscles of his legs twitched beneath my fingers. He put his hands on my head and entwined his fingers in my hair.

I had no need to switch on my instant arousal love button this time. The slickness between my thighs was natural, my arousal my own. I let go of his leg and touched myself gently, not wanting to move too fast.

"Have you won awards for this?"

The question so startled me I let him slide out of my mouth with a moist noise. How could I ever have mistaken Declan for a Pleasurebot? The humor sparkling in his dark eyes was too human to be mistaken for anything else.

"Do I deserve one?"

In reply, he tugged me to my feet and kissed me again. Brief regret flashed through me at how I had almost never known the feeling of his mouth on mine, that I'd denied him access to my lips before this, when I could have felt him kissing me. His hands splayed around my hips, and he lifted me.

I am not a small woman, but he didn't even stagger as I wrapped my legs around his waist. Now my head was higher than his, his mouth was at my breasts, and he took the time to give them equal attention. My nipples tightened beneath his questing tongue. My head lolled back, the fall of my hair once again providing exquisite sensual counterpoint to what he was doing with his mouth.

Somehow, we landed on the bed, Declan between my parted legs. It was like landing in a cloud, pillows and blankets and softness all around us. He moved up a little, just enough to push himself against my opening. Then he stopped.

I opened my eyes. "What's wrong?"

"Are you sure you want to do this?"

I could have smacked him. "Declan!"

He laughed and buried his face in the sensitive spot beneath my chin. "Just asking."

"Now?" I wriggled beneath him. "What more do you want?"

His mouth teased flesh of my throat. "I want everything."

I didn't ask him to explain. I was afraid to learn his words were only sex talk—or perhaps equally as afraid to learn they were not.

In reply, I lifted my hips again, just enough, and he slid inside me. I bit back a low moan, but Declan didn't bother. He let out a low, shuddering sigh against my skin, and I felt the brief pressure of his teeth on me. I tensed, waiting for pain, but none came. He nipped softly, then laved the area with his tongue.

He set a slow, gentle rhythm. I met his thrusts with my hips, my legs hooked over his calves, my arms around his back and his face buried in my shoulder. We rocked together that way forever and for but a moment. Time meant nothing in the sensual haze of delight our lovemaking was creating.

Sparkles of climax burst within me, built and burst again. We murmured words, but I don't know what they were. He smiled as he pressed his forehead to mine, our eyes locked together, our bodies moving in perfect time.

I know I wept, and wasn't ashamed of my tears. Declan licked them away, and I tasted the salt of my emotion on his tongue when he kissed my mouth. We joined and parted, every movement like a choreographed dance, until I could no longer keep myself from crying out his name as my body surged toward a final orgasm.

"Gemma," he whispered, the sound of my name like music on his tongue.

I gave in to the pleasure, let it take me, sweep me away. The pace quickened and his breath grew harsh in his throat. He shuddered as his climax burst from him, and I joined him in the trance of sensuality overtaking us.

I slept beside him in that soft bed, and woke to find myself alone in the dark. Beside me on the pillow lay a red rose. A real flower, not hologram. I lifted it to my nose and inhaled the true and beautiful scent of it, and I touched the pillow where his head had rested.

He'd also left a note.

TONIGHT.

CHAPTER 6

I moved through the next morning as though I'd been wrapped in plastic film. Colors and sounds seemed muted and hazy. I couldn't stop myself from smiling at inappropriate times.

I had another date. We were going to an outdoor show at one of the larger city parks. He'd asked to see me again, and while the thought of it made my stomach clench, it also made my heart pound so fiercely I imagined the world could see my blood pumping through my body beneath my clothes.

"Hey, Gemma." Eddie snapped his fingers in front of my face. "Wake up."

"Sorry." I focused my gaze on his face. "What did you say?"

"I asked which District you wanted to patrol today." Eddie peered at me closely. "You all right?"

I nodded. "Sure."

He touched a spot on my neck, exposed by my regulation upswept hairstyle. One of Declan's love bites, still sensitive even today. "What's this?"

"I saw him again."

"Who?"

Eddie's a great partner and a helluva sexy man, but he is, after all, a man. Sometimes you have to lead them a little bit.

"Declan."

He frowned, still not getting it. "Who's he?"

I sighed, but couldn't get too frustrated with him, even if I was going to have to spell it out for him. "IIP."

"Shit, G! What were you thinking?" He looked so stunned, I almost laughed.

"I wasn't on duty. It's okay."

We were currently the only passengers on this stretch of the pedtread. Eddie still looked around surreptitiously, like someone could overhear us. An unlikely event, in any case, since the Newcity motto is "to thine own business attend."

"You didn't file that report."

I shook my head.

"G!" Eddie grimaced. "If Rando finds out…"

"She's not going to find out." I gave him a stern glare. "Is she?"

He held up his hands. "Not from me."

I hesitated before telling Eddie the rest of the story. Eddie's been my best friend for four years. But he is a guy. Guys do not always understand the importance of things like flowers—or at least their ideas of why symbols like that are important are a whole lot different than women's. Still, he is my best friend, and with Britney still gallivanting around Offworld, I had to tell someone.

"He asked me out. I have another date with him tonight."

Eddie didn't say anything for a long couple of minutes. He only stared. The silence between us had almost become uncomfortable when he spoke.

"Good for you, Gemma," he said quietly. "It's about time."

We were on duty, so he couldn't hug me, but his gaze wrapped me in the warmth of his friendship. Tears stung my eyes for a moment before I blinked them away. "Thanks, Eddie."

He tapped my shoulder, the highest level of physical affection we could show on duty, and gave me one of his patented grins. "See what a mind-blowing orgasm can do to a person?"

I gave him a punch on the arm, a lot harder than the one he'd given me. "Let's get to work."

Because we were working in pairs, our patrol area was twice as large. We'd been assigned Sector 1, which included Districts 26-32, 51-56 and 76-100. Newcity is divided into four Sectors and one hundred Districts, all arranged in a series of concentric rings. We'd have to cover a lot of ground before tonight. Eddie grumbled as we headed toward the first Lovehut, but without much heat. He loves his job. I'm just good at mine.

"Let's start with the huts and move to the clubs," Eddie said. "Get through the registered bots before we go after the unregged ones."

That sounded fine to me. Even this early in the afternoon, the Lovehut was packed. They all have state-of-the-art beverage and food service, all the sports channels on the viddy and even reading material. They've become the most popular recreation facilities in the Newcity, even if you're not looking for sex.

Of course, most people in the 'huts are looking for sex. Even if they come for any other reason, like to watch the latest Entron-8 versus Halitopa intergalactic Donball match on the viddy, it's likely that before the night is through they'll be engaged in some sort of sexual congress. STD's were eradicated about 75 years ago, and all citizens are provided with completely effective birth control that has to be surgically reversed in order to procreate. Without the fear of disease or inadvertent pregnancy, citizens have made sex the number one favorite recreational activity. It even beats viddy watching.

Eddie and I both spotted a likely subject at the same time. She was a tall, statuesque brunette. She didn't really look much different from the statuesque redhead or blonde standing beside her, but what gave her away was the quiver. Ops learn to spot it from a mile away. A Pleasurebot with a faulty ignition shivers when she smiles. It's a subtle gesture, but one that can't be hidden, since it's programmed into them to smile almost all the time.

It can be nearly impossible to tell if a bot's about to malfunction, but with this one there could be no doubt. She was so far gone even a citizen should have been able to tell she was ready to explode.

Not the guy chatting her up, apparently. Or maybe he was one of those people who get off on the danger of it. More likely, he thought he could handle it. He had that over-muscled, macho look about him: bulging arms in a too-tight shirt, thighs like pillars. His neck was so thickly corded you could have played a tune by plucking his tendons.

The brunette looked like a PSSN-F-03 to me, but after my recent mix-up I felt myself second guessing. Eddie had no problem. He gave the couple a nod, and said in an aside: "Passion Model, looks like an 02. Definite quiver. You want to take it, or should I?"

I prefer het pairings, though of course I'll do whatever the job requires. Since I had the choice, though, I was more than happy to give this one to Eddie. Watching and standing backup would be fine with me.

We walked over to the brunette and her partner. The man instantly blanched and looked from us to her and back again.

"Shit," he said.

"Sir, step aside, please." Eddie took a little too much pleasure in usurping muscle-boy's date. It was that testosterone thing, I guess. I could practically smell it on both of them.

The guy knew better than to protest, though, as I'm sure he would have had Eddie been a civilian. The uniform gets a lot of respect, especially since the penalty for assaulting an Op became instant Offworld jail time. Offworld prison isn't pretty.

"R.I. Op EDDE 08111977." Eddie lifted the sleeve of his shirt to show off the tatbadge. "Registration, please."

The brunette gave him a wide-eyed stare. Her lips trembled. She was trying desperately not to smile. After a second, though, her internal programming won out over free will, and she flashed her pearly whites. The instant her lips curved, her cheeks and eyes began a minute series of tremors which lasted for about two seconds. The quiver.

"I have my regs right here, Officer." She unzipped the top of her one-piece jumpsuit and exposed a set of firm, full breasts topped with cherry nipples. She lifted out a small pouch and handed it to Eddie.

He remained unmoved by the sight of her bare chest. Off duty Eddie can be hornier than a moose, but on the job he's purely professional. It would take a little more than bare boobs to get him worked up.

Eddie glanced at the small selfcontained viddy unit, then handed it to me. Her name was Relava, manufactured fifteen years previously. I gave her another look. She was in pretty good shape for her age. Most Pleasurebots who aren't in private service get worked hard. Her skin was still pretty, her eyes still clear. Aside from the broken ignition, she could have walked off the assembly line last week. Okay, maybe last year. The closer I looked, the more wear and tear I saw.

"Is there a problem, Officers?"

At least she wasn't going to run. "Your inspection is out of date, Relava. We have reason to believe you have a malfunctioning ignition. According to Mandate 6978, we're going to have to check you out."

She sighed and looked so broken for a minute I thought she might cry, except bots have no tears. "Okay."

We took her to the closest station, only about a block away. She gave us no trouble, but no help, either. She didn't say one word the entire walk.

We signed in and went to one of the sterile white rooms. Without being asked, Relava unzipped her jumpsuit and stepped out of it. She folded it carefully and put it on the dresser. She was conscientious. Someone had taught her that. Most bots just toss their stuff right on the floor—they're careless by nature.

"How long were you in private service?" I asked.

She looked startled. "Four years. I was a pre-order."

Eddie gave me a glance. It was hard not to feel sorry for these metalgirls. Somebody had looked through a catalog or browsed online, chosen their features and personality traits, clicked a button and placed an order. It was harder for them than the generic off-the-shelf models. Pre-orders had higher expectations made of them.

Eddie began to read her rights. "I am going to engage in sexual congress with you. You will perform appropriate sexual acts with and upon me in order to stimulate me and yourself to orgasm. Am I clear?"

She nodded. She looked at me. "Is she going to participate?"

"Operative GMMA 03271971 is going to observe and assist if necessary."

I knew what Eddie's idea of assisting was, and I stifled a chuckle. It must be every man's fantasy to have two women at once. I pulled up a chair and sat to watch the action.

"I'm sure Operative EDDE 08111977 won't need any assistance from me."

Relava shrugged. "Okay."

I'm sure she didn't feel much like smiling, but she had no choice. My heart went out to her again as I watched the quiver cross her lovely features. If we found she had a faulty ignition, and I was certain we would, Relava would have to go in for repairs. A model this old would be unlikely to be released back into the workforce. It was more likely she'd simply be donated for Offworld prison use, or sent to one of the Oldcity sex centers. She might even be retired.

Relava went to Eddie and knelt in front of him. With her eyes on the floor, she sighed so fiercely her creamy shoulders lifted. Then she reached for his crotch.

Eddie put his hand on hers. "Wait, Relava."

Again, the wide-eyed stare. "You don't want that?"

Eddie, still fully clad, looked at me over Relava's head. I could tell he was as sympathetic to this bot as I was. She didn't have much of a chance, poor thing, and her behavior showed she knew it.

Eddie, despite being a testosterone-driven man, is also tender-hearted. "Get on the bed, Relava."

Her perfect brow creased. "Okay."

Eddie shrugged out of his shirt and pants, and tossed them to me to fold. I'd say men are also careless by nature. Maybe that's why bots are, too—they were designed originally by men, after all. I set his clothes and utility belt on the dresser, though I'd make sure to give him a little hell later about his assumption that I'd perform maid duties.

Eddie has a fine body, without cosmetic enhancements. He keeps trim through workouts, not surgery. The hair on his body is slightly darker than the hair on his head, and it furs his chest, arms, legs and groin. He's a tall man, too, with long legs and a long torso which combined make him seem taller.

He's also got an amazing penis. It's not huge in length or girth, though I know many women find that attractive. It's just the right size. What makes it so extraordinary is its perfection. Every ridge and wrinkle is lovely, from the pink, smooth head down to the thin-skinned surface at the root. Eddie's cock tastes like spice—not musky, not dirty. He's always clean.

Watching him, even though at this moment his penis still curled in its nest of hair, flaccid, I felt myself stirring. I could too well remember what sort of lover Eddie is, and thinking of it made my body recall Declan's touch and the way he made me come.

A faulty ignition won't break down until after the second orgasm. Eddie had his work cut out for him. Relava lay back on the bed, legs spread. Clearly she wasn't expecting much in the way of wooing.

Eddie is a quality, not quantity, man. It's the reason he's so popular with the ladies in his personal life. He knelt between Relava's open thighs and touched her, gently, just inside each knee.

"I'm not going to hurt you." It might have sounded trite or clichéd, but Eddie meant it. Not all Ops uphold the tenets of our training: be generous in your duties. Most hold the Newcity motto in higher esteem. "To thine own business attend." It doesn't make for good lovemaking.

Pleasurebots don't require much foreplay—they're programmed for pleasure and can come from stimulation that would leave a normal woman cold. But just because they don't need it doesn't mean they shouldn't have it. Their sole purpose is to feel and provide pleasure, and anyone who doesn't allow them that is doing himself a huge disfavor.

Relava relaxed against the pillows. Eddie slid down the bed until he lay prone, propped on his elbows, his face between her legs. From my vantage point I could see everything he was doing. Technically, I didn't have to watch…I just wanted to.

Her pubic hair was limited to a fluffy tuft just above the hood of her clitoris. Below that, around her labia and anus, she looked as smooth as satin. Her clit was like a ruby red jewel tucked into a tiny cloak of pale peach. Now, because of Eddie's attentions, it pushed up from its covering. She glistened already, the dew of her arousal coating her opening.

Eddie pushed her legs flat to the bed and met my eyes in the headboard mirror. He was doing that so I'd have a clear view. That devil. He knew me too well.

He bent his head to Relava's waiting clitoris and licked it. She made a low moan, and her hips jerked. I could imagine all too well the sensation pulsing through her. I felt it answered in the twinge between my own legs. Since I wasn't expecting to participate in this inspection, I hadn't bothered to press the button which would turn on my sexual response receptors. Then again, I didn't think I'd need to. Watching Eddie go down on Relava was enough.

She sighed. "That's nice."

Like I said, it doesn't take much to please a Pleasurebot. They can get off if the wind blows the right way. Eddie was making a little more effort than that.

With slow, regular strokes he swept his tongue along her cherry red button. Regularity was the key. Too many men think if they stagger the strokes it will get us hot faster. Eddie knows better.

He worked his tongue a little faster while he stroked her thighs. I could see the glisten of her sex fluids, and my own vagina clenched in response.

From my vantage point, it was easy to see how Eddie's cock was lengthening and stiffening. It pushed against the softness of the mattress, and he lifted his hips to allow it room to grow. Now he went up slightly on his knees, his erection standing along the line of his belly like an arrow pointing to Relava. His balls tightened and relaxed while I watched, and the sight made my breath catch in my throat. He was so lovely.

The curve of his buttocks, lightly covered in golden hair, prompted me to reach out and caress him, but I resisted. I was on the job. There was to be no personal pleasuring in an inspection station—and this was Eddie's inspection, not mine. Watching him lick and stroke Relava made me think of Declan, and how he'd done the same to me the night before. How could I help getting aroused?

Eddie slid a finger inside Relava, and she let out a small yelp of pleasure. As he slid it in and out, twisting his hand so his finger twisted inside her he continued the same regular licking of her now hugely engorged clitoris. Relava was making mewing sounds. Her thighs trembled, and her hips jerked with every stroke he gave her. It wouldn't be long before she had her first orgasm.

Eddie's cock twitched against the sheets and his buttocks clenched as he thrust a little bit. He'd fuck her next, because it was the best way to get a bot to malfunction if she were going to.

Relava's mewing turning to a low, continuous moan. She arched back, bringing her flesh up to meet Eddie's mouth and hand. The bed shook from her tremors. She cried out, then again, and Eddie pressed his finger deep inside to trigger a deeper orgasm. She came, head thrashing, hips jerking, thighs splaying.

"That was really nice," she said after a few seconds. She smiled. The quiver was more noticeable now. "Now do you want me to go down on you?"

For people outside the field, it's hard to understand how your body can be straining with sexual arousal but your mind can remain calm and professional. What they don't see is that sex for Ops is a job like any other. Athletes use their bodies in their art, and we use ours. If you don't learn to separate the job from your private life, you'll never make it in the field. R.I. Ops rarely orgasm on duty, even though we might be aroused.

"You will perform fellatio until I tell you to stop." Eddie's penis bobbed a bit on the word fellatio, but his voice was steady. "You will self-stimulate as appropriate. Do you have any questions?"

She shook her head, and they switched places on the bed. Eddie leaned against the headboard, with Relava between his spread legs. Without hesitation and frankly, without much finesse, she lowered her mouth onto his erection. Eddie closed his eyes for a moment as initial sensation must have rocketed through him. He didn't make any noise.

Relava took in his entire length, then let him slide almost all the way out. Then she got down to the rhythm of sucking him off. Her hand slipped up to cup his balls, and her thumb stroked him along the line of skin between his anus and testicles. Eddie's jaw clenched.

It is harder for the male Ops than for the female. Women are just naturally better at separating themselves from what their bodies are being asked to do. It's probably a defense trait to cope with things like menstruation and childbirth. Since becoming mecho, I am unable to do either one.

What Relava lacked in creativity she made up for in enthusiasm, aided by her hand between her legs. She lifted her rear in the air while she put her fingers inside herself and busily masturbated. She was already moaning. Her buttocks flexed as she moved against her hand. The cry she made was muffled with her mouth still wrapped around Eddie's penis, but still audible. She'd had another orgasm. I sat up straighter in my chair, watching for signs Eddie might need help in subduing her.

"Now I'm going to perform sexual intercourse with you, vaginally." Eddie motioned for Relava turn around. "We're going to begin in the male from behind position."

Relava's eyes were glazed. She still smiled. Now the skin on her face jumped and ticked, still in a way that untrained eyes would pass off as flirtatious expression. To me it boded trouble.

Now Relava faced me on her hands knees, with Eddie behind her. He took a breath, probably to clear his head, then pushed his length into her. Even though she'd had two previous orgasm, Relava let out another low moan of pleasure. She couldn't help it. She's programmed to love fucking.

Eddie put his hands on her hips and set up a slow, teasing pattern of strokes that had Relava quickly pushing herself back against him. Eddie maintained the pace, but after a few moments, it no longer mattered. She went into overdrive.

She'd put her head down low, so I could only see the top of her head. Now she flung her head back so fast and far the white curve of her throat met my gaze. Maybe she was trying to speak, or to scream. What came out of her was a hideous, low grinding, the sound of rusty gears gone too long without oil. Relava's back hunched even as she continued to thrust herself on and off Eddie's erection. Her body shuddered as her hands clenched the sheets so hard they came off the bed.

Eddie looked grim, and sweat broke out on his forehead. "She's going over."

"You got it?"

He nodded. "She's in clenchdown."

"You're in for a helluva ride, Eddie."

Clenchdown was an unfortunate autoresponse to an ignition on the fritz. She'd clenched her vagina down so tightly on Eddie's cock he wouldn't be able to pull out until she finished....or was inactivated.

We'd trained for this lots of times, but it's different in real life. In training, you know you're not going to get hurt. In the field, nothing is monitored. Nothing is safe. This bot could ride Eddie until he broke and then keep fucking his corpse for hours. Or she could just constrict his dick so forcibly she popped it off like a cherry from its stem. Either prospect wasn't pretty.

Eddie barely flinched. The muscles on his arms stood out as he gripped her pounding hips. "I'm going to try and get her to come. Maybe she'll calm down."

"Or maybe she'll get even more fired up." I patted my stunner. "I'll cover you."

"Thanks, G." Now his voice revealed some of the strain he was under. Agony and ecstasy warred on his face for a moment before he smoothed his features again. "She's a wild one."

Relava bucked against him. Her smile never faded. Her hair had begun to tangle from all the head tossing.

Eddie reached around and found her clitoris with his index and middle fingers. The instant he touched her there, Relava yelped and shuddered. He pressed against her again, and she came again. Her hips never stopped moving, thrusting against him, pulling him in and out of her. Fucking him in overdrive.

"She's not stopping," I said. Watching her still fascinated me.

Eddie shot me a glance that said he knew damn well she wasn't stopping. He grabbed both her hips again. His own thrusts were becoming ragged.

"I'm close," he muttered through gritted teeth.

"Really?" I was surprised at first, then not. Relava was really giving him a ride. He wouldn't be human if he didn't get off on it.

Eddie gave me another one of his looks. "When I'm done, you pull her off."

We'd have a few scant seconds when Eddie's semen might override the clenchdown. Pleasurebots are programmed to release at the presence of ejaculate. I wasn't hopeful this one would. She was too far gone.

It shouldn't have been sexy to see Eddie being fucked like crazy by a bot out of her mind. But it was. Any man on the verge of orgasm looks totally hot. The way his eyes closed, as though he couldn't keep them open. The way his mouth thinned as he tried not to moan. His chest muscles rippled, followed by the hard, smooth planes of his abdomen. A man this close to coming is sheer perfection.

I positioned myself at their sides, and wrapped my arm around

Relava's waist. Her skin was hot, practically burning up. She rolled her hips, probably trying to arch her clit toward my fingers, but I wasn't cooperating. I held her harder.

Eddie made a familiar low noise. I glanced over my shoulder. He was going to come.

When he growled, I yanked. At first nothing happened except that Relava and Eddie both hollered at the same time. I yanked again. Relava and I both flew forward and ended up in a tangled heap on the floor. I was up in an instant, but she didn't move. She remained, crumpled and twitching. The strong stench of ozone and something burning filled the room. She was smiling.

"I've got her secured," I called back to Eddie, as I slipped the stuncuffs loosely over her wrists. She didn't move. "But…I think she's done."

Eddie wiped himself clean and got dressed with swift efficiency. "We'll have to take her in."

I nodded. "Another life saved."

He punched me lightly on the shoulder. "Better me than some poor, unsuspecting sucker, right?"

"Yeah."

I watched Relava stir. Coherence returned to her eyes, and she looked at her bound wrists.

"Okay," she said. She'd stopped smiling.

CHAPTER 7

Whatever passivity had been programmed into Relava's nature was quickly overcome by the instinct of self-preservation. As soon as Eddie and took her out of the Inspection station, she ran. I'm ashamed to say she caught me by surprise, but my thoughts were of the seeing Declan that night and not on making sure the bot in my custody didn't escape.

Before we even got to the pedtread, Relava drove her stiletto heel into the side of Eddie's calf. Our boots are designed to prevent such injuries of our feet, but she got him just above the top of the boot. Right in the muscle. With a curse that echoed off the buildings around us, Eddie went down. She didn't wait to see if I'd help him or go after her; she just took off.

A human woman running with bound hands and wearing stiletto shoes would have tripped herself and fallen in moments. Relava, however, had the advantage of permanently arched feet and perfect balance. She also had the advantage of never tiring.

I left Eddie writhing and bitching on the sidewalk and ran after her. My feet had to slap the pavement twice as fast as hers just to catch up, but I'm in shape—and I'm mecho. I have enough tendon and sinew made from indefatigable materials to keep me going longer than unenhanced citizens.

Relava, however, had me beat. Her break was so unexpected she had the time to get a good head start, and desperation fueled her. She dodged through the growing crowd as we crossed Districts. Hardly anyone looked twice at the half-clad, stuncuffed woman fleeing in their

PASSION MODEL

midst, though I got a few sideways glances as I passed. I couldn't get close enough to her to use my stunner.

She zigged, and then she zagged, and ducked into an alleyway I'd never have noticed if she hadn't shown me with her flight. The crowd parted, but barely, and only when I screamed at them to move, move, move! By the time I got to the alley myself, Relava had disappeared.

I couldn't even hear the sound of her feet pounding the pavement. I looked up, thinking she might have crawled up one of the concrete walls, but still saw no sign. Wherever she'd hidden herself, it was good.

"Damn." I put my stunner back in its loop on my belt and rubbed my temples. I was going to have a helluva headache when Rando got wind of this.

By the time I exited the alley, Eddie had managed to limp up. Blood stained the navy uniform a dark violet. He'd wrapped a strip of bandaging from his first aid pack around his leg, and the blood there was bright red against the cream gauze. Seeing the blood and Eddie's murderous expression, the crowd gave us a wide berth.

"She got away?" Eddie asked.

"Yeah." I jerked my thumb toward the alley. "Down there."

He peered over my shoulder down the shadowy corridor. "Ahhh, Rando's going to have a field day with this one. We messed up, G."

I nodded. "We didn't know she'd run, Eddie."

He gave me a look. "You think Rando's going to care?"

"No." I urged him away from the main traffic area and closer to the wall. "Let me look at the wound."

He leaned against the building, and I bent to lift his trouser leg. The puncture her heel had made was deep and nasty looking. It had already begun to clot. It needed more attention than a sloppy bandage.

"We need to get you to a medstation."

Eddie shook his head. The crowd's curiosity had passed, and people moved in front of us on their way to the pedtread without a backward glance. Attending to their own business, like good Newcitizens.

Eddie shook his head. "We need to find that bot and take her in to a repair station. If we don't, Rando is going to go nuclear on us."

"We're not the only Ops to lose a 'bot, Eddie."

"That's the point, G. Rando is furious with this coming on the heels of those Ops using the Inspection Stations for private assignations. The whole Academy is coming under fire for incompetence, and she's not going to let her Department have any slack."

He was right. I unsnapped my own medkit from my belt and took

71

out the tube of antibacterial gel and a fresh pad of gauze. I peeled off the bloody bandage and ignored Eddie's muttered curses when the material stuck to his skin. Then I cleaned and rebandaged the wound. I couldn't do anything about his bloodied uniform leg, which had already begun to stiffen.

He must have been feeling better, because he gave me a lascivious grin when I got to my feet. "It's been a long time since I saw you kneeling at my feet like that. Maybe you should get back down there."

"Dream on, Eddie." I smiled. "You couldn't handle me anymore."

He put a hand to his heart and made a fake grimace. "Ooh, that hurts."

"You'll get over it." I repacked my medkit and used a squirt of alcohol gel to clean my hands. "Where do you think she went?"

Eddie reached down to rub his leg, then straightened. "I'm guessing she went to ground. That's what they usually do."

That meant making the rounds of the kennels. It would take hours. We didn't have much choice. If we went back to the patrol station without an arrest to report, Rando would have our heads.

"Check her stats. See where she's registered," I said.

Eddie glanced over the small viddy screen she'd left behind. Then he let out another muffled curse. "She's regged in every District in Sector 1."

Bots in public service often did that so they could have a broader home range. Since they couldn't go more than 48 hours without returning to a kennel for recharging, registering in more Districts gave them more flexibility. The problem was, Newcity has 100 Districts. Each District can have anywhere from 10-15 kennels, depending on its size.

"We could get lucky," I offered. "Find her in the first one."

Eddie lifted his leg and shook it at me. "Do you feel lucky? I don't."

The good mood I'd been nursing all day slowly dissipated when I realized how long this search was probably going to take. Suddenly, I didn't feel so lucky either.

*   *   *

It made sense to start with the kennels closest to where I'd lost her, but Eddie and I didn't think Relava would have sought shelter there. She was a bot on the run. Her sense of self-preservation would have sent her as far from the perceived threat, us, as she could get before she had to recharge. That meant we had to head over to District 56 first.

"We don't have time to pedtread, G."

I nodded, and tried to pretend my stomach hadn't just leaped into my throat. "I'll be fine."

"I'll try to get one that doesn't go too fast."

"Eddie." I shot him a look. "The only hovertaxis that don't go fast are the ones ready to break down. I think I'll take my chances on the speed."

He patted my shoulder. "You'll be okay."

I forced a cocky grin I didn't feel. "Hell, yeah."

The truth was, I couldn't ride in a hovercraft without breaking into a sweat. My hands shook, my throat constricted, panic set in until I thought I might faint. I avoided them whenever I could.

"At least we don't have to follow her Offworld." I made a feeble attempt at a joke. I couldn't get in an outer atmospheric vehicle. I went practically catatonic from terror. I'd undergone three years of counseling, only for the therapist to determine my "irrational" fear of motorized craft stemmed from my accident on Solaria. No shit. I quit therapy and used the pedtread.

Eddie hailed a passing hovertaxi. As soon as I saw its distinctive blue and green stripes, I had to swallow. Hard. Nausea warred with the cold sweats to overpower me. I fought them both back with a series of mental exercises Kaelyn had taught me. They helped…a little.

"District 56." Eddie paused to read Relava's records. "Brenda Kitten's SexKennel."

The driver, a bald Dieselian with tattooed, bulging arms, looked over his shoulder. "Fare in advance."

Eddie and I slid up our sleeves to show him our own tattoos. Meager in comparison to his plethora of inkings, but more powerful. He gave me a smirk and turned back to the controls.

"Sorry, Officers," he said. "Didn't know it was you."

"Submit a bill to Department 42," Eddie said. "You'll be reimbursed."

"Yeah, yeah," the driver said. "I know the drill."

I couldn't say anything at all. I concentrated on my exercises. Breathe in. Hold. Breathe out. Hold. Picture a lovely place, a happy place. Breathe in. Breathe out. What worked like a charm for the Keanicans required a lot more work from me.

With a whir that dropped my stomach from my throat to my toes, the hovertaxi lifted. It moved smoothly into the stream of traffic, and I was grateful for that.

We got to Brenda Kitten's SexKennel with no incidents. Eddie held my hand, tight, the entire way. He's a great partner, but he's a better friend.

If the Vindieselian thought anything strange about two Ops holding hands like love-struck teeners, he didn't say anything. His gaze met mine in the rearview mirror, and he nodded, almost imperceptibly. When he lowered the craft to its resting place, he spoke.

"Must have been a real bad accident."

I shouldn't have been startled. Dieselians know better than anyone else about the aftereffects of accidents. They are, after all, a race which prides itself on scars.

"It was."

He nodded again. "You take care, now."

His sincere comment took me aback for a moment. "Thanks."

I watched him for a minute as he sped away. When did people start surprising me again?

Brenda Kitten's wasn't one of the fanciest kennels I'd ever seen, but it was clean and well-run. Brenda herself met us at the front desk. Her eyes flickered at our uniforms and our tatbadges, but she didn't try to stop us from entering.

"I ain't seen her," she did say. "You can look, but she ain't here."

We didn't take her word for it. Eddie and I went down the dim corridor and searched the communal dressing area. The room was quiet. All Pleasurebots are programmed for small talk and idle chatter—but when they're alone they don't bother. They have nothing to talk about with each other. Several units sat in front of the dressing table mirrors, and others rifled through closets of sexy outfits. Though the room had several comfortable couches, the only bots who sat on them were those putting on their shoes.

Eddie cornered an auburn haired PSSY 75 struggling into a latex dress. "We're looking for one of your sisters."

She stopped struggling long enough to look at the holophoto in Relava's ID unit. "Sorry."

Eddie tapped her shoulder through the thin dress. "Look again."

The bot gave the picture an even less impressed look, if that were possible. "She's a Passion Model."

"We know that," I told her.

Eddie wasn't so patient. "Just look at the holo."

She gave it a third, equally uninterested glance. "I think I did a ménage with her last week."

I put a hand on Eddie's arm to prevent him from losing his temper. "We need to know if you've seen her today."

"No." The PSSY 75 went back to smoothing the material of her dress over her thighs. "But she could be in one of the booths."

After the violently orgasmic half an hour she'd spent with us, Relava would definitely need recharging. The question was, had she chosen Brenda Kitten's kennel to do it in?

All kennels are laid out the same way. From the communal dressing area, several corridors branched off. One led to a bathing room, with multiple shower heads and minor repair facilities. Pleasurebots don't eat, so they don't need to eliminate—but they do need to bathe. Tables with tools they'd need to fix minor malfunctions and injuries lined one wall. The other corridors, four in the case of Brenda Kitten's, were lined with a dozen each small doors. Booths. They were the reason these recharging stations had come to be known as kennels. Walking down the row of booths was just like walking through the old animal shelters where people used to go to find pets somebody else hadn't wanted. Dog and cats had become a thing of the past, but people still kept pets. Some of them kept Pleasurebots.

Each booth's door was made of slightly tinted plazglass. It was easy to see which ones were occupied. Inside each booth, padded armrests and neck supports, along with a three-pronged recharging stud made up the entire contents of each booth. The bots simply stepped inside, attached their USB ports to the outlet, got comfortable, and recharged. It was the closest thing to sleep they experienced.

Checking each booth wouldn't be difficult, but it would be time consuming. We decided to split up. A bot recharging in a booth isn't able to easily escape. Eddie took the first two corridors.

The first two booths I checked were empty but for the faint scent of ozone. The next had a blonde occupant. She smiled at me as I peered in. No sign of a quiver, thank the astros.

The next was a brunette, also a PSSN but probably an F-07 instead of an 03. Still, her features at a casual glance could have passed for Relava's, at least through the tinted plazglass. I thumbed the door release, and it slid open with click. The bot's eyes hadn't been closed, merely unfocused. Now she blinked. And smiled.

"Hi."

I showed her my badge. "I'm looking for a PSSN-F-03, street name Relava."

"Okay."

"Do you know her?"

A shake of the head. Perfect lips pursed. "Sorry. No."

This close, I could see this wasn't the bot I was looking for. "Sorry to bother you."

"Okay."

The door slid closed, and I moved on down the corridor. None of the bots in my two halls were Relava. One said she might have seen her earlier today. Another had ménaged with her at a local Lovehut the night before.

"Was she showing any sign of malfunctioning ignition?"

The TITS-777 I was interviewing swiped a tongue along her lips. "Nothing that bothered our client."

"But she was malfunctioning."

The TITS, whose street name was Shaedo, didn't answer for a moment. "She was an older model. Yeah, she could have used some upkeep, sure. Who can't?" She gestured to her own perfect body. "Some of us take more pride than others. Some of us are just better made."

There's a definite caste system among Pleasurebots, understandable only to themselves. While regular citizens might have their preferences with models and physiques, one Pleasurebot tends to be treated the same as any other. Among the bots themselves, it's a different story. The smarter ones look down on those with less installed RAM. The ones with specialty features like anti-grav, removable limbs, or additional inputs roll their eyes at more conventional bots. I guess everyone needs something to feel superior about.

I noticed a telltale dark spot on Shaedo's otherwise perfect inner thigh. "You do realize that I am also authorized to detain and inspect bots I suspect might be renegade for any reason—not just malfunction?"

She probably couldn't be scared, but my veiled threat had made her a little nervous, at least. Her fingers, tipped with nails the color of platinum, fluttered near her thigh but didn't touch the dark spot. "I know that."

I looked very deliberately at the discoloration, which could have hidden a private ownership mark—or not. "For instance, bots who jumped the private sector before their contracts were up. If I asked you to show me your ID unit, Shaeqdo, what would it say?"

She lifted her chin. "Relava nearly blew a gasket last night, okay? But the client was ready for her. He had special equipment, so went she went into clench down he wasn't caught."

Special equipment. It could be something as simple as a latex sheath, something like the condoms men used to use, that would let the client's penis slip free of Relava's clenching muscles. There were other things too. It didn't really matter.

"He hired her knowing she was malfunctioning?"

Shaedo shrugged. "Paid us both twice the hourly fees to keep our mouths shut." Her fingers fluttered over the dark spot again. "Don't ask me to tell you who he was."

"I'm more concerned about finding Relava. She's going to hurt someone if she doesn't get repaired soon."

Shaedo already knew the worst. "She's too far gone for that. Unless somebody buys her for themselves, she's going Oldcity or Offworld. And she knows it, too."

A bot who knew her future would be even more desperate. "See you around."

Shaedo licked her lips and gave me a sultry stare. "I hope so."

I ignored her flirtation. She couldn't help it. I couldn't be flattered or offended by it.

Eddie hadn't had any luck with finding Relava, though he'd met up with a bot who had seen her earlier today at the Lovehut we'd detained her in. That was the closest we'd come. With twelve other kennels in this District alone to search, we needed to get on the move.

Kennels are divided into three types, convents, monasteries and dual gender facilities. As their names implied, some housed only female bots, some only male, and some both. It was unlikely we'd find Relava in any of the monastery kennels. At least that would cut out some of the work.

"Where to next?"

"Whiteknee's." Eddie named the second biggest kennel in this District.

Luckily for me, we could take a pedtread, not a hovertaxi. We hopped a tread and reached Whiteknee's in about ten minutes.

We had no better luck there. It had the same layout as Brenda Kitten's, but all the bots we checked there hadn't seen Relava recently. Most claimed to never have seen her at all.

"We're getting colder," Eddie said, outside the kennel. His stomach rumbled. "I'm starving. Rando's going to have our asses if we don't find her before next shift."

My stomach growled too. "We're in the right District. I can sense it.

It's out of character for a bot to go to ground too far from her registered home District.

"Call up the map, G."

"This is why you love working with me, isn't it?" I grumbled, but pressed the spot on my temple that activated my internal downloads.

"No, I love working with you because you can get a bot off in under three minutes," Eddie said. "You boost my productivity ranking."

I had to laugh. The holomap streaming from my eye sockets jiggled for a minute. "Shut up. You'll make me fritz the map."

Eddie stabbed the air in front of the map. "Here we are. There are thirteen kennels in this District. Four monks, four nuns and three orgies."

The map was complete and updated every four seconds. It flickered as we watched, then renewed power. We appeared as two glowing blue specks on the darker gray of a sidewalk. Whiteknee's glowed a faint red. I blinked twice, hard and shifted the view toward the next closest kennel.

"K.C. Rogers' Kinkhouse. Think she might have gone there?"

Eddie nodded. "Most of the other bots we interviewed said they'd ménaged with her, so we know she's available for other than just vanilla pairings."

I tapped my temple again and brought up the Kinkhouse specs. "It's also registered as having a larger repair and maintenance facility."

"It caters to the rough trade. If she's going to attempt a self-repair, that's a likely spot. Let's move on it."

The crowds cleared out of our way as we got closer to K.C. Rogers', which was funny to watch since the people in that area looked a hell of a lot scarier than either Eddie or I. It's interesting to see how our uniforms make even the baddest of black vinyl clad and piercing-riddled citizens give us wide berth. It proves the Ruling Council right on at least one count—intimidation and the threat of swift and harsh punishment is a better deterrent against crime than weapons could ever be.

I'd rarely come to this part of Newcity before. Bots that service the rough trade are used so hard they don't usually last long enough to become a problem. I wasn't unfamiliar with the sorts of acts which went on in this part of town, though. SMBD is not my personal preference, and as an officer it was unlikely I'd ever have to participate in anything like that during an inspection, but I'd been trained in them just the same.

Even the Lovehuts in this part of the District reflected the taste of their clientele. More viddy screens showed hard core sex videos than sporting events, and the drugs listed on the sidewalk menu boards included some of the heavier, more potent cocktails. Not for the beginner. That stuff would knock you on your ass for a week if you weren't used to it. Painkillers, pain enhancers, muscle relaxants and paralyzers—a veritable cornucopia of chemicals to make your body do things it normally didn't want to.

"Up there." Eddie pointed to the discreet silver and black lettered sign that stood over the Kinkhouse door. The house symbol was a black stiletto pump, outlined in bands of pulsing silver. Pretty classy, compared to some I've seen.

Once inside, I could see why. The Kinkhouse proprietor was as classy and sleek as her sign. Long sheaves of brown hair fell past her shoulders. She dressed simply, in a form fitting gown of black artisilk and shoes that matched the sign outside. If our appearance stunned or unnerved her, she showed no sign of it.

"Good evening, Officers," she said in a pleasant contralto voice. "How may I be of service tonight?"

"We're looking for a bot."

Her gaze flickered toward Eddie, and her subtly painted lips hinted at a smile. "My kennel houses some of the best in Newcity."

"We're here on business. Not pleasure."

Now she turned her gaze on me. "Of course. How may I help?"

Eddie showed her Relava's holophoto. K.C. looked at it with narrowed eyes, then shrugged.

"I don't recognize her, I'm afraid. She might not be one of my regulars."

"But she could have come here. She's registered in this District." I watched her carefully for signs she might be sheltering Relava, but saw none.

K.C. nodded. "I assume she's been having...problems?"

"Malfunctioning ignition. She ran from us when we tried to take her in for repairs." Eddie seemed entranced by K.C.'s cool gaze and calm demeanor.

"I see." K.C. tapped slim fingers on her counter. "A bot like that could be very dangerous."

"We'd appreciate access to the kennel," I told her.

Again, she nodded. "You realize, of course, that a bot with that propensity for danger would likely be highly prized in this part of the

District. It's probable she's engaged in congress right now."

"If she's not recharging we suspect she might be attempting self repair of the malfunction." I put my hand, not as subtly as Ms. Rogers, on my stunner.

"Of course." She pressed a button and the door behind her slid open smoothly. "Be my guest."

The communal area was done in the same silver and black décor as the lobby. Racks and baskets of vinyl and plastic accessories dominated the space. All manner of Pleasurebots, including the relatively rare VCTM models, prepared themselves for the evening.

"Haven't seen one of those in a while," Eddie said with a nod toward one of the VCTM's.

She had slash marks all over her naked breasts and belly. Unlike some of the other models, who were busy repairing the minor blemishes their violent activities created, the VCTM was only patting on thin layers of plazskin over her wounds. Any amount of pressure on the slashes would reopen the cuts immediately—which was just the effect she wanted.

She glanced at us from mismatched eyes, a sign she'd been through some heavy action that had required some more major repairs than the ones she was making now. She was exactly the sort of bot whose clients might seek out a damaged PSSN model.

"We're looking for a PSSN-F-03, street name Relava." I showed her the holo.

She spoke in a voice like grated glass. "I don't work with regular bots."

Despite what most people might think, the VCTM models are actually among the most intelligent. They have to be. Dumb bots putting themselves in situations where they're caused constant physical harm as part of some citizen's sexual thrills would be destroyed so fast it wouldn't be worth constructing them.

"She's got a damaged ignition."

"Well, that changes things." She gave the holo another look. Her flat gaze took in the picture, and then she nodded. "I've seen her."

People expect Ops to be taciturn and steadfast all the time, but when we get a break we get just as excited as anybody else. I maintained my composure better than Eddie, who let out a long, hissing "yesss!" The VCTM gave him a jaded glance that reminded me how much some of these models are really like women.

She pulled a complicated contraption of spikes and vinyl from a rack and looked at it for a moment before slipping it over her breasts. The spikes, instead of pointing outward, dug into her skin. She didn't flinch.

Intelligent or not, she obviously still needed leading. "Where did you see her?"

Luck had finally caught up with us. She jerked her head toward one of the corridors. "She was recharging back there a while ago."

Sometimes, my instincts scare even myself. Before I even turned, I knew Relava had entered the dressing room. Her high heels chattered on the floor, the quiver had become so pronounced.

There's not much loyalty among bots. The ones gathered in dressing room scattered like rats startled by the light of a hovertaxi. Relava didn't waste any time. She shot through the room, shoving the VCTM model aside with one arm, and barreled through the room at top speed.

Eddie was quick, but I'm just faster. Relava flew past him. Her eyes met mine for one startled minute, and then she was past me, too. I whirled in place and followed.

She pushed through the doors and into the lobby, and I was close enough on her heels to smell the stench of ozone that clung to her like bad perfume. I swiped a hand at my stunner, but she put on an extra burst of speed as we rounded the edge of the desk and I couldn't get close enough to her to reach.

In another moment, she hit the street. The plazglass doors cracked behind us, but we kept going. Relava lurched through the crowd, which had become larger as night fell.

I switched easily into hyperdrive with nothing more than a mental push. The muscles and tendons in my legs took energy from organs getting less use at the moment, like intestines and kidneys. My lungs expanded the extra fraction that allowed me to take in extra air. I pushed off from the pavement. I'm not truly able to fly, but in those moments of hyperdrive, it's as close as any person can ever get. My hand swiped at her and caught the trailing strands of her dark hair. My fingers tangled, and she stumbled.

It wasn't quite enough to stop her. She kept going for another few feet, right into the path of traffic. The hovertaxi screeched to a stop, but not soon enough. The vehicle struck her, hard, in the midsection.

Her torso split, and her limbs separated from her body. Her head rolled along the ground. She was still smiling.

Blue sparks arced for a moment between the sad, scattered pieces of her body before fizzling to black smoke. A finger twitched, and one eye closed. As quickly as that, she was deactivated.

"God-of-choice, I hate doing a Blade Runner," I muttered. My stomach twisted.

The crowd didn't pause to gawk. The hovertaxi driver got out and inspected the front of his undamaged vehicle, asked me if he needed to stick around, and cursed when I told him he's have to fill out some paperwork.

Eddie appeared with a tarp from inside, and we waited until a cleanup crew arrived to pick up the pieces. That and the inevitable forms we had to fill out took a good part of an hour, and by that time, darkness had fallen over this part of the District.

Eddie clapped a hand to his stomach. "I'm starving."

Relava's flight and demise had stolen my appetite. "Let's call it a day."

"Hey, G," Eddie said with a glance at his timepiece. "Didn't you have a date tonight?"

The world seemed to stand still for a moment. I checked my internal clock. "Oh, no."

I'd forgotten all about Declan.

CHAPTER 8

It was too much to hope he'd waited for me. Torn between wanting to shower and change or rush straight to the park, I opted for the latter. The park was dark when I got there, the show long over and even the last lingering lovers disappearing to other pursuits.

I gripped the metal fence with fingers gone numb with disappointment. Even though I scanned the grounds of the small area with my night vision, I knew I wouldn't register Declan. I forced my spine to stiffen. There was no sense in falling to pieces.

Newcity never sleeps, but I'd never longed for empty streets and dark alleys more than I did now. I didn't want to mingle in the groups of citizens heading for their evening's entertainment. I only wanted to go home, get undressed and wash away my frustration beneath a stinging hot shower, synthetic water or not.

The minute the door to my apartment slid open, Kaelyn fluttered up to me. "My Gemma looks tired."

"I am tired, Kaelyn."

She cocked her head to look at me. "I programmed the steam shower for my Gemma."

I grasped her slight arms and kissed her cheek. "You are a treasure."

Her face pinked with pleasure. "My Gemma looks sad, too."

"Did…did anyone call for me here tonight, Kaelyn?"

Her fine features crumpled in concentration. "No."

I hadn't thought another surge of disappointment could fill me at her answer, since I'd expected it, but my already low spirits sunk further anyway. I couldn't be surprised. Declan probably thought I'd stood him up. Why would he have bothered to call me?

I put my soiled uniform in the disposal unit and paused at the interdomicile supply port to order another for the next day. The viddy display showed Kaelyn had already taken care of it for me. I wasn't exaggerating when I called her a treasure.

My fingers brushed the keyboard but didn't push any keys. I didn't know Declan's code, or his District, or anything more about him than the scent and taste of him. He knew where to find me, but I had little hope he'd do so. How long had he waited? Not long enough and I couldn't blame him.

The steam shower responded to the warmth of my body and switched on as soon as I stepped into the plazglass enclosure. Instant heat seeped into my body. The steam wrapped around me, and needles of nearly scalding water pounded my flesh. It was just what I needed.

Kaelyn waited for me outside the bath room with a glass of synthfruit juice and a slab of some sort of fragrant cake. "I ordered this for my Gemma."

Even my disappointment couldn't take away my sudden appetite. It had been hours since I'd eaten, and I'd worked hard today. I gobbled the food and drink, gave Kaelyn the plates, and ran my internal ultrasonic tooth cleanser. Then, still naked, I coated myself with waterproof protective dreamcream and got into my water bed.

The curved metal lid closed over top of me with a low, comforting click. Darkness instantly bathed me, and silence cloaked me. The water adjusted rapidly and perfectly to my exact body temperature, which had elevated slightly after the steam shower. I put the mouthguard between my teeth and plugged my ears, then slipped the duel-pronged flexicord into my nostrils and felt for the switch that would turn on the oxygen. The first two seconds of forced air were as stale and shocking as always, but then it was as though I were breathing regular air.

I slipped down into the water. Floating. The water caressed me, held me, lifted and dropped me, all as gently as a mother crooning her child to sleep. The slap, slap of it against the inside of the bed had the rhythmic quality of the sea.

I floated, aching for sleep and not finding it. No matter how I tried to tell myself it was stupid to pine away over a man I barely knew, my mind kept returning to his face. The way he whispered my name. The feeling of his hands on my flesh.

I floated. Thinking. Yearning. Would he try to see me? What would I do if he didn't?

I'm an Op. It's my job to find out who and where people are. With my access to Newcity's database, System, it shouldn't be difficult to trace Declan. The truth was, I was afraid.

No person had ever affected me this way, not even Steve. My ex-husband's face rose briefly in my mind, but any memories of the love we'd shared had been replaced with the sight of his face on the viddy screen the last time we'd spoken.

His lip had curled in disgust, and his eyes hadn't quite been able to meet mine. He'd asked for money, and I'd refused. I hadn't asked him why he'd decided to dissolve our union. The answer had been all over his face.

It was too soon to imagine sharing my life with Declan the way I'd shared it with Steve. Yet I couldn't stop my mind from turning over a picture of us, laughing together. Holding hands. Standing before our friends and family to share the vows that would join our lives as husband and wife. Loving him.

I had loved Steve once, enough to agree to bind my life to his. His touch had made my body respond. We'd even laughed together, though it seemed I only ever cried alone. If I hadn't agreed to join him on the hoverbike ride, perhaps we'd still be married today. We might have had children.

That choice had been taken from me. I'd never create life or carry a child in the womb the doctors had determined unimportant to save. Compared to the organs which allowed me to live, lungs, kidneys, intestines, I suppose their choice made sense. But now I pressed my hands against the flat plane of my belly and imagined the scarred mess inside.

In our world's past, motherhood had once been assumed to be the sole purpose of a woman's life. Her role was to create, bear and raise children. Time had allowed women more freedom of choice, but motherhood had still been considered the shining icon of womanhood, the pinnacle of purpose for the female sex. More recent advances had further removed that assumption. Same sex pairings, artificial insemination, and birth control reversible only by surgery had made having children more of an active choice than ever before. Women can choose to have a uterobot carry the egg and sperm joined in a laboratory rather than become pregnant themselves. We can choose our children's gender, hair and eye color, genetically determined height and weight, resistance to disease and aptitude for tasks.

I still had choices. Too many of them in my opinion, but I could still be a mother if I chose. But I didn't want a child without a father, and I didn't want a home without love.

I wasn't afraid to make love with Declan, but I was afraid to love him. I'd gone down that path before, with Steve, and had my love torn from me like meat in the teeth of feral beasts. The accident had stolen more from me than my internal organs, it had taken my marriage.

I floated, dreaming. I couldn't maintain the melancholy thinking of Steve and my accident always brought me. The water soothed away those old aches, which is why I invested the money in the water bed to begin with. No matter what befell me during the day, no matter what might wound or scar me, sleeping in the water, the real water, always made everything better.

I spread my legs to feel the water caress every part of me. In the silence, the beating of my heart became the thud of ocean waves. I thought of my holo program, and the blue ocean I'd created.

In the blackness, I couldn't be sure if my eyes were open or shut. Soft sparkles of color drifted through my vision, like tiny stars. If I reached out my hands to either side, I'd feel the warm inner lining of the water bed, but I chose to keep them resting on my stomach. I wanted no tether, nothing to ground me. I wanted to float, to drift, to let the day slip away from me.

Despite the warmth and gentle rocking of the water, I couldn't relax enough to fall asleep. Tension coiled through my body, my thighs, my shoulders, my neck. I stroked the smoothness of my belly and felt the tension even there, muscles jumping beneath the skin.

The situation with Relava preyed on my mind. She hadn't needed to be destroyed, but desperation had driven her recklessness. She'd lost her life because of her own fears. Still, my responsibility in the fiasco preyed on me.

My hands smoothed lower, to the swell of my thighs. The muscles there ached, but the warm water would relieve the pain by morning. My fingers touched the sensitive inner flesh, and the skin there trembled at my touch.

If I'd met Declan tonight as planned, we surely would have ended up making love. His hands would have touched me where my own caressed me now. I let my fingers drift a little higher, to brush the soft lines of my vagina and the swelling bud of my clit. I closed the third finger and thumb of my left hand on that spot. Just behind the bundle of nerves was the switch which forced my body into instant sexual arousal. I didn't need to press it. My touch against my flesh and the thought of Declan was enough.

I parted my legs further, and the water lapped at my openness. I rocked my hips against my hand. The stars in my vision grew brighter, sparkled, pulsed in time to the throb of my arousal.

I slid the first two fingers of my right hand inside my opening and felt the slickness even the water couldn't wash away. My hips jumped, and my clit began to heat. I moaned in the back of my throat, the mouthpiece muffling the sound. I slid my fingers in and out, deeper, harder, imagining them as Declan's cock. My other hand stroked my clit in slow, rhythmic circles that brought me to the edge, then eased me back.

The water sloshed. My knees bumped the sides of the tank as I drew them up to tilt myself further against my hands. I thrust my fingers slower, and slid my left hand up to caress my jutting nipples. The water licked at my erect clitoris, teasing it, taunting it. No matter how I pushed against it, the pressure wasn't enough to send me into orgasm. I teased myself with it until my body became a blast of sensation, and even the stars in my eyes faded into a white hot glare.

At last I could hold out no more. I left my breasts and slid my hand once more down to my center. Once, twice, I tweaked the bud of flesh with my thumb and forefinger, and my orgasm bolted through me hard enough to arch my back and slap the water against the tube. I waited a second or two, and paused in the stroking and thrusting, then once, twice, again, and a second, milder series of contractions rippled through me.

Spent, I let my hands fall to my sides. The water calmed. I floated. Then I slept. If I dreamed, I don't recall it.

*   *   *

My internal clock woke me, and I slid seamlessly from sleep to consciousness without the startlement that so often accompanies the change.

I pressed the rubber button and removed the flexicord and other gear. The lid of my water bed slid back to reveal a room, dim in deference to the blackness to which my eyes had grown accustomed, but still bright enough to make me squint briefly. I felt no sense of urgency, and for a moment couldn't think why. Then it struck me. Today was my scheduled off day.

For a moment I sank back into the water, but couldn't stay there for long. I couldn't recall the last time I'd taken a day of leisure. My job had been life for so many years, even the idea of actually staying home on my off day for any reason other than an emergency seemed like craziness.

The more I thought about it, the better it sounded. I got up from my water bed and wiped off the dreamcream, then tossed the towel in the disposal. I stretched, the tiny joints in my back popping and crackling. Yesterday's strife and disappointment seemed shoved far back in my brain, and today stretched out in front of me with colors glowing like Solaria sunshine. Bright.

"Is my Gemma going to work today?" Kaelyn's fair head peeped around the corner. "Is my Gemma feeling sick?"

"I'm not sick. It's my day off."

Her brow furrowed. "But my Gemma does not take her day off. She always goes into work anyway."

"Not today." I gave myself a glance in the mirror. "Today I think I'm going to…relax."

She probably wouldn't have looked more aghast had I said I was going to eat filth. "My Gemma is sick!"

I laughed, and drew her closer to me. "No, Kaelyn. Just…I've been thinking. Life is too short."

Her wings fluttered against my bare arms. "Is it something I've done wrong? Is my Gemma going to send me away?"

My heart twisted a little at her assumption that any change in me was a reflection of her status in my household. I smoothed her hair gently away from her forehead and held her still until her wings ceased their beating. "No, Kaelyn. I'm not going to send you away. I would never do that. I love you."

The dark fathoms of her eyes brimmed with tears. She flung herself against me, shaking with the force of her emotion, and I realized something that shamed me. I had never told her I loved her before.

"Oh, I'd hoped and hoped, but I never thought my Gemma would…oh!"

I rubbed her back, feeling through her light shift the thin knobs of her spine poking up in the space between her gossamer wings. She clutched me harder. I held her for some long moments, neither of us speaking.

When she pulled away, she seemed almost shy. "When my Gemma bought me from the slave trader, I was afraid. Many of my people have died at the hands of yours."

"I know that." I let her stand back from me. "I don't like it."

She nodded, and her delicate features wreathed into a smile. "But my Gemma has been so kind, never working me too hard. Caring for me. They took me from my home when I was very small. Away from my family." She paused as if to consider her next words. "I've thought in my heart, felt in my heart, for a long time…"

"Yes?" I prompted her.

"I wondered if my Gemma treated me so well because I cost much money, or because she loved me as I loved her. Because I've lost my mother, my Gemma, and…"

Tears stung my own eyes as her words sunk in. "Oh, Kaelyn. I didn't realize."

She nodded again. "My Gemma doesn't want me to think of her this way. I understand!"

"No, Kaelyn." Again, I drew her close to me, this time so I could look deep into her eyes. "For a long time, I couldn't feel much of anything. But I've always cared for you. And I'm honored that you feel for me what you did for your own mother."

The petite winged creature I'd bought for three month's salary had no idea of the gift she'd just offered me. "I'd be honored to have you as my daughter, Kaelyn."

She threw herself at me again and wrapped her arms around my neck. She hugged me so fiercely the air squeezed from my lungs, and I had to pry her off. She stepped back, her wings for once ceased in their constant fluttering. She looked more serene, and her eyes shone with a glow I recognized as happiness.

She drew away and clapped her hands. "I will make my Gemma…" Again, the shy pause. "My mother, breakfast."

I laughed and shook my head. "All right."

With a flutter, she left the room. I stared after her for a moment. I had a Keanican for a daughter. I grinned. Stranger things had happened.

Again, I dressed in a flowing dress of soft artisilk and slipped flat sandals instead of heavy boots on my feet. I made a quick diagnostic check to be sure my internals were still functioning—unlike the hapless Relava, I placed a lot of importance on my personal maintenance. If something went wrong inside me, it would be far more serious than a simple faulty ignition. In the unlikely event any of my organs failed, I'd die. It seemed a fair trade for never being sick.

Today I would put the past behind me once and for all, including Steve. I'd look forward to what the future might bring. I would start by finding Declan.

* * *

I would never know if I had a chance at a future with Declan, if I didn't try to find out. The thought of telling him the truth—that I was neither metalgirl nor fleshgirl, but something in-between, made the pit of my stomach clench. The fear made me angry, and made me think. How long had I allowed it to rule me?

In my work, I was fearless. I had to be. And in my private life…well, because of fear I hadn't allowed myself to have a private life.

"No more," I said. Yes, I thought of the way he'd made my body sing, but more than that, I thought of how he'd opened my heart.

There was always the possibility that once he learned the truth that I was mecho, he might turn away, as Steve had. As so many of the Newcitizens were beginning to do, led by the Newcity Ruling Council. I'd never know unless I found out. And I wouldn't find out, unless I found him.

I still didn't want to go into work, but with my home hookup to System, I wouldn't have to. I barely noticed the plate of soft bread, articheese and synthfruit Kaelyn slid in front of me, though when she clucked at me to eat, I did. I unhooked the viddy screen and keyboard from the wall and put them on the table for easier access. With luck, my search wouldn't take very long, but I wanted to be comfortable.

I punched in my personal ID number and waited for System to recognize me. When the modulated feminine voice replied, "GMMA 03271971, recognized," I replied, "voice command activated."

"Activated."

"Search: Declan."

The viddy screen showed a flowing, random pattern of colors for approximately two seconds before a list of matches appeared. The system was working incredibly slow.

"Match: Declan. Two million, three hundred thousand, four hundred and seven."

"Damn." I thumped the table. I hadn't thought his name would be so popular.

"Command not recognized."

"Discard: All but first of multiple references."

Again, the soft pattern of blues and greens, then the list of names.

"Match: Declan. Seven hundred and two."

At least I'd cut the list down considerably. I hadn't even reached the point where I had to use my higher clearance to gain information.

"Discard: Female."

"Match: Declan. Five hundred and seventeen."

Now I was getting somewhere. All of the remaining references were of a male Declan, and each was a reference to a different event. Now all I had to do was figure out which one was the one I needed.

"Filter: Social refs."

"Hold or discard other data?"

"Hold." If I couldn't find the correct social reference to him, I might need to check business.

I'd finished my breakfast without paying attention. Kaelyn cleared my plates, her eyes still shining with the glow of joy. She hummed softly to herself and paused to lay her head against mine before moving back to the kitchen area.

"Match: Declan. Social. Three hundred and fifty."

"Filter: Photos."

"Hold or discard other data?"

"Hold." I waited. Finding a picture of him would make everything else much easier. The answer came back.

"Match: Declan. Social. Photos. Seventy-five."

"Show first match."

A brief splash of color, then the screen filled with the face of a very handsome man. It wasn't my Declan. The man's toothy grin graced an advertisement for the Ultra Sonic Tooth Cleaner.

"Identify Citizen."

"Offworld Citizen. D'clan Horduta."

There was a problem with voice recognition technology. It wasn't System's fault, but the ad didn't help me. I ordered another match, this time spelling out the proper name.

"Match. D.E.C.L.A.N. Social. Photo. Two hundred and four."

At least the numbers were getting smaller.

The clip showed a man accepting an award for something, and shaking hands with several people. I scanned the background for a sign of my Declan—now I was starting to sound like Kaelyn! But saw nothing familiar. The words marching across the bottom of the screen matched described the scene.

"Volume up."

"...Frank Phillips accepts the Newcity Good Citizen award from Newcity Council Member Howard Adar.

The dialogue continued. "...Frank's work with Oldcity plague groups earned him the award."

The clip faded. "Reference entry. Declan?"

"Further information unavailable."

"Replay."

The clip began again. I scanned the background. "Stop." I touched the viddy screen lightly. "Enhance."

The dark head I'd spotted was turned too far to make out the face. I tried again, several times, enhancing the images of several figures in the crowd, without luck.

"Stop. Enhance."

The eyes. The set of the mouth, the arc of the chin. They belonged to a much younger man, but were still unmistakeable. It was my Declan.

It was difficult to speak through my sudden grin, but I managed. "Stop. Run Citizen profile."

"Citizen profile unavailable."

The smile slid from my face. "Run Citizen profile."

The answer hadn't been a glitch. I asked another question. "Query. Profile restricted or deleted?"

A deleted Citizen Profile would mean Declan was into crazier things than seducing on-duty Ops. Only criminals took the extreme efforts required to delete the profile which every single Citizen accumulates since birth. I didn't want to think about what that would mean.

"Restricted."

Now here was a puzzle. I ran the clip again, from the beginning, and though. I touched the viddy screen on Howard Adar's face. "Citizen Profile."

"Partial Citizen Profile available."

"Run it."

"Howard Frecious Adar, Citizen ranking 100,000 level. Son of Richard Adar, Newcity past Ruling Council Leader. Leader of Ruling Council for the past forty years. Married for forty-five years to Cyndira Winston Adar. Four natural children. Kantsta Adar Bullock, daughter. Farquinn Adar Lazar, daughter. Larden Adar Horat, daughter. Caldyx Declan Adar, son."

"Reference. Caldyx Declan Adar."

"Citizen ranking not applicable. Son of Howard Frecious Adar and Cyndira Winston Adar."

The profile continued, listing his siblings, education and

accomplishments, but I barely heard the rest.

Declan was an Adar. He was the son of Newcity's most important Ruling Council Member. And, as far as I could figure out, he'd died six years ago.

CHAPTER 9

Six years before I had paid no more attention to the news of the youngest Adar's misfortune than necessary. With every viddy screen in Newcity blasting the broadcast repeatedly, it would have been impossible not to notice the story—but six years before I'd been living my own merciless existence in post-surgical rehab. Learning to walk again, to breathe and eat on my own, to speak, had taken up all of my time.

Caldyx Declan Adar had been driving his custom designed holocycle along a deserted Calypigian beach, when a monstrous, irritable beast called a Thudjid, maddened by his proximity to her nest, rammed him. He'd lain in the sand for hours before family members noticed him missing from their vacation compound. When they finally discovered him, not even their vast amounts of wealth could buy his life. Or so the news stories said.

I was beginning to suspect a different truth. I knew all too well the stigma attached to becoming mecho. I'd lost a career and a marriage to it. How much more devastating would it be to a family as revered as the Adar's? A family in which every member was held up as an example of perfection to the citizens of Newcity? People might forgive indiscretion and shady behavior, but not scars.

I sat back in my chair and stared at Declan's face. Instead of death, he'd become mecho, and they'd hidden him away from society so as not to tarnish the family name. Surgery had changed his features enough that not even the ever-present media had figured it out.

Had he been a willing participant in the charade? I had to think so, at least at first. To a young man whose entire life had revolved around being recognized, lauded and imitated, suddenly becoming the object of thinly veiled disgust would have been too much to handle. "To thine own business attend" didn't apply to the family which was the closest thing Newcity had to royalty.

It had been horribly difficult for me, and I was a mere common citizen. At least I had the advantage of being able to keep my condition a secret to strangers—he would not have had that option. Living in the public eye would have exposed the truth before his stitches had healed.

Yes, I could see how Caldyx Declan might have agreed to remain hidden. But no man, no healthy, intelligent man, could possibly bear isolation for long. No amount of money could replace a life. He must have decided to risk discovery.

"System, match: This Citizen," I tapped the face on the viddy screen, "photos only."

The picture faded, and a series of thumbnails popped up. I tapped the first. Declan in the background again, his smile brilliant enough to shine even in the crowd. I tapped the next thumbnail, and a similar picture came up.

"Busy boy," I murmured, quickly viewing the first ten listed. In every one, he was in the background of some party, some function or sports event. Never the subject of the photo itself, and never, other than the Frank viddy story, mentioned in context with the Adar family. He'd been careful about that.

I let System idle while I thought. Kaelyn fluttered around me until I told her to find something on the viddy to watch. She loved banal game shows I usually restricted as too annoying, so with a squeal of pleasure she went to the living room to gorge herself on the stupidity.

What to do now? More than ever, I determined I had to see him. Since I had a pretty good idea now of where I might find him, the only question was whether or not I had the guts to do it.

Seeking Declan out now meant more than opening my heart—it likely meant risking my job. If Howard Adar learned I'd discovered his family's dirty secret, it might even mean losing my life. I had no doubts that one mecho R.I. Op would be no loss compared to the Adar family reputation—at least, not in Howard's eyes. I also had no doubt he had the capability and the opportunity to remove the possibility of any embarrassment, including me.

I peeked in on Kaelyn, happily ensconced in her favorite chair, eyes glued to the viddy screen. A woman screamed as she was told she'd just won an all expense paid trip to New Bermuda. The other contestants looked glum as the electric shock equipment was hooked up to their foreheads.

"What are you watching?" I paused to ask.

"A dancing show." Kaelyn giggled. "Watch them dance."

As she spoke, the losers of the game did start to dance. They danced so hard some of them began to smoke. I changed the channel to a less violent show, one where the losers only had to perform a humiliating feat rather than be physically harmed.

"That's not a good show, Kaelyn."

"My Gemma doesn't like dancing?"

I patted her head. "Not that kind."

She gave me a quizzical look. "My Gemma's people are strange. On Keani, we don't have competitions."

I hadn't known that. "No games?"

She shook her head. "We all win."

I couldn't say I liked that any better than the show she'd been watching, but at least it wasn't violent. "Kaelyn, I'm going to go out, after all."

"To work?"

"Sort of."

She frowned, then sighed. "All right, my Gemma."

I thought of something. "Would you like to go out?"

Her fine features crumpled slightly. "Out?"

I thought of Declan, forced to remain in hiding. "Yes. Outside. To the park, maybe, or to eat at a restaurant?"

Kaelyn dissolved into frightened tears. "No, oh, no! My Gemma, are you angry with me? What have I done?"

She clutched my ankles until I bent to lift her up. "No, I'm not angry. Why would you think that?"

Her tears disturbed me. I wiped them away and rocked her in my arms until she quieted. Her hair was the texture of fine silk, and smelled of spice. Her cheek was hot against mine, and wet with her tears.

"You would make me go outside?"

"You don't want to go outside?" I'd never asked her before.

She shuddered. "Oh, no. Someone might steal me away from you. It's too big out there. And it smells."

For a small Keanican, used to a world full of nothing but beauty and peace, I could see how Newcity would be frightening. And she was right. Somebody might steal her. But I didn't want her to be a prisoner. I had bought her, in the eyes of the law she was my property, but I did not own her.

"I just thought you might be tired of being in here all the time, that's all."

"Not when my Gemma comes home to me every day."

She nestled closer to me, her tiny hands like curled birds against my dress. She felt no heavier than a bird must have been, and I closed my eyes against the sudden ache of mingled joy and grief in my heart.

What would happen to Kaelyn, I wondered, if something happened to me?

*   *   *

Few of the citizens on the pedtread met my gaze. It wasn't that they ignored me, exactly. More like, when I put on the dark blue uniform, they simply didn't see me. Unless they needed me or wanted to avoid me, I was a nonentity.

That anonymity would work to my advantage even more today, when I planned to access parts of Newcity in which I really had no jurisdiction. The Adar family, all of them, resided in a residential District surrounded by several blocks of security space. Technically, Newcity had outlawed segregation, voluntary or not, a century ago. Reality, as always when dealing with the wealthy and privileged, was different.

There are few places in Newcity where the pedtreads don't run. You can even, if you're so inclined, ride the treads all the way to Oldcity and beyond, to the empty land. Some people take day trips despite the discomfort and danger, to catch a glimpse of real earth and genuine sky. All tread routes ended, however, when the security space around the Adar's home res-dist began.

I saw no warning signs and heard no alarms. The family was more subtle than that. The pedtread simply ended, its woven metal construction disappearing tidily into its slot in the pavement where it would travel underground back to its beginning and resurface for another journey.

I stepped onto the deserted concrete. It was quiet here, with nothing more than a low humming to disturb the silence. Quiet, and clean, a further indication traffic here was light. The street and the sidewalk both continued past the low plazbrick wall which indicated this as a non-res District. I didn't see any thing to stop me until I stepped past the wall.

97

"This District restricted to foot traffic." System's modulated female voice purred from hidden speakers. "Please retreat or face security measures."

Security measures could mean anything from a mild electric shock to complete system alert. I wasn't going to risk that. I stepped back to the other side of the wall, searched for the telltale black square which indicated the System access box, and spoke.

"Query. Hovertraffic accepted?"

"Affirmative."

System only answered the questions I asked it—it wouldn't extrapolate. "Query: next District restricted?"

"Affirmative. Next District requires class A Security Clearance."

I had that. "Query: Next District security clearance?"

"Restricted. Class A with further clearance codes and retscan required."

"Command: summon hovertaxi to this location."

"Command received. Citizen responsible for payment upon arrival of unit."

My gut clenched at the thought of riding in the craft, but I was determined to end the day by finding Declan. In just a few minutes, a familiar face leaned out from the hovertaxi window.

"Hey, pretty lady."

It was the scarred and philosophical Dieselian who'd taken me and Eddie yesterday. For some reason, the sight of him calmed me enough to slip into the back seat without sweat breaking out on my forehead. I leaned forward to let his retscan unit clear me and deduct the credits from my account.

"Where to?"

I pointed ahead. "Through there."

He cast a glance over his shoulder. "You got security clearance?" He looked up and down my body, then grinned. "Yeah, I guess so."

The craft moved smoothly forward, and I sat back in the seat. The security space was empty, concrete, devoid even of plantings which could beautify it. The message was clear: this place was not for pleasure. It had nothing to do with normal citizens. Anybody here better have a good reason.

My reason might not pass inspection for the Adar primogenitor, but it was good enough for me.

"Never been in this part of the city." The Dieselian met my eyes in his rearview mirror. "What you looking for?"

"I'm looking for someone."

His throaty chuckle probably tumbled women into bed at the sound of it. "This someone part of the ruling family?"

Diesela still has a monarchy. Though technically Newcity is a democracy, his terminology wasn't incorrect. He knew the importance of the Adar family.

"Maybe."

"You're not gonna tell me."

I had to return his grin. "Nope."

He shook his head as he guided the taxi around several concrete pillars. "Just like a cop."

"Warning: Security clearance required."

Once we drove through the pillars, the hovertaxi's power cut out. The vehicle slid to the ground. The Dieselian shrugged, helpless.

"All up to you, now."

I got out of the vehicle and met the two secbots rolling out of their guard posts. I held up my tatbadge and opened my eyes so they could scan me.

"State your business."

They don't bother making secbots humanoid. All they need is speed and strength, and that can be better gained with wheels and multiple limbs. Even their voices are harsh and metallic, designed to intimidate. I'm not easily intimidated.

"I have an appointment with Declan Adar."

A harsh whirring sound issued from the secbot to my right. "Citizen does not reside in this District. Please return to your craft."

"Caldyx Declan Adar," I amended.

Now the secbot on the left spoke up. "Citizen does not reside here. Please return to your craft."

Secbots can't lie. They'd been programed not to know Declan still lived here. Howard and the Family had taken every precaution.

"I have Class A Security Clearance. I have an appointment with a member of the Adar family, who do reside in this District."

Whirring, then a click. "Appointment not recorded. Return to your craft."

"You want me to leave?" The Dieselian asked from through his window.

I waved him on. "Thanks for the ride."

"You sure?" He sounded doubtful. "I don't want to leave you here…"

"Go ahead." I faced the secbots squarely. "I'll be fine."

"You take care, pretty lady."

The hovertaxi moved smoothly away and left me alone with the secbots. They whirred and clicked menacingly. The red laser points of their visual circuits swept up and down my body. Checking for weapons, probably. I'd left my stunner at home.

"Access denied."

"I have Class A Sec Clearance," I repeated patiently. Secbots are strong, not smart. "Statute 5734756-49-XB states Citizens with appropriate Sec Clearance may have access to areas requiring that level of clearance without previous appointment."

They whirred and clicked some more, but couldn't really balk me on that one. The statute was obscure and rarely enforced. Citizens with high sec-clear are usually the ones smart enough to know where not to tread.

"Statute activated. You'll be escorted."

"Fine with me.

Security around the Adar complex was clever. What appeared to be a continued empty lot disappeared when we passed through a sec-shield strong enough to leave sparks crackling along my fingertips. The faint scent of ozone tickled my nostrils.

We stood in a richly decorated foyer. Floors of inlaid wood, probably real and very expensive, met walls hung with luxurious draperies. A large closed door stood at the room's opposite side.

"Wait here."

The secbots slid back through the nondescript door through which they'd brought me. I waited. I touched one of the wall hangings. It felt like real silk. Even the air smelled like wealth.

After a moment, an elderly man appeared in the opposite door. He looked perfectly human from the waist up, but instead of legs, he was equipped with a square platform and two flexible treads. The treads rested on multiple moving pieces, which would allow him extreme maneuverability and the ability to climb stairs.

"Madame wishes to see...?" The servebot waited politely for me to finish.

"Caldyx Declan Adar. Please," I added as an afterthought.

The bot looked sorrowful, a neat trick since I was certain he wasn't programmed for emotion. "I regret to inform Madame that Master Caldyx is no longer with us."

"I regret to inform you that I know that is untrue," I replied calmly.

"And if you won't take me to see him, I'll see Howard Adar instead."

The bot gave me a pained grin, another false emotion. "I regret to inform you that Master Adar is unavailable to the public at this time. Should you care to make an appointment…"

"Dursely, stop." A male voice I recognized drifted from the doorway, followed a moment later by its owner. "I'll see her."

It was Declan.

* * *

He took me through a series of rooms more exquisite than I'd ever seen, even on the viddy screen. He didn't speak, or look at me, and I had to be content with staring at the back of his head. My heart sunk, and I thought I must have made a serious mistake, but it was too late to back out now.

He finally took me to a small room equipped with a comfortable couch, a large viddy screen, and several shelves of outdated self-contained entertainment units. He motioned for me to sit, while he went to look out the small window. I chose to stand.

"So now you know the truth about me." He turned to face me, finally, and the beauty of his features made my throat close.

"Declan…"

"You might as well call me Caldyx." His tone was bitter. "It's my real name."

I couldn't do that. To me, he would always be Declan. "Declan. I'm sorry I didn't make it to the park the other night. I got caught up in an arrest."

"And you just happened to find out where I live. Who I really am."

"I didn't just happen to. I searched for you."

He ran a hand through his hair. His face looked bleak, his cheeks scruffy and eyes red rimmed. "I don't blame you for not wanting to be with me."

I took an involuntary step toward him. "How can you say that?"

He pointed at his chest, and disgust twisted his face. "Now you know the truth. I'm mecho."

"Didn't I tell you scars don't bother me?" I tried to smile, though his attitude was making it tough. "Declan, I'm more surprised to learn you're an Adar."

Now he finally looked at me for the first time since my arrival. "Gemma, I'm not proud of that, either."

I reached out a hand, but the way he stepped back made me drop it back to my side. "I wanted to meet you. I got caught up in a job. When

I got to the park, you'd gone. I waited for you to contact me, but you didn't. So I started looking for you."

He laughed, though he didn't sound amused. "Sure you did. I waited four hours, until I got the holonote."

I hadn't had time to send a note. "I didn't…"

Again, he didn't wait for me to speak. "I should have died in that accident, but I didn't. And when I finally decided to pick up the pieces and try to gain some semblance of a real life, I didn't realize how hard it would be. People…they look at you differently if they know you're mecho. You can be metal, you can be flesh. You can even be enhanced. But to be mecho is something else so completely different. It shouldn't be, but it is."

At his words, hope stirred inside me. "I understand."

He fixed me with a glare. "You can't possibly."

"Not about being part of the most powerful, wealthy and influential family in Newcity, no." I tried to force him to meet my gaze, but his eyes skittered away from mine.

He sat on the couch, face in his hands. "Gemma, the night I met you was the first time I'd slept with a woman since the accident. I've been out for over a year, but I've never gotten that close before. When you mistook me for a Pleasurebot, I figured it was some sort of irony. But then…"

"Then what?" I prompted him.

"Then I couldn't stop thinking about you."

I sat next to him and put my hand on his shoulder. "I couldn't stop thinking about you, either."

His back shook beneath my touch as he let out another series of humorless laughs. "I saw your face when you noticed my scars. I know how people feel about mechos. I don't blame you for being disgusted."

Before I could tell him my own secret, he pushed away from me and began to pace the small room. When he finally whirled to face me, the look on his face made me cringe. "What I don't understand is how you can do this to me?"

He'd left me behind. "Do what? Try to find you? To explain why I missed you that night?"

He lifted his chin and gave me a cold grin. "You had to do some pretty fancy research to figure out who I am. I've been damned careful."

"Not that careful," I shot back. Now I was getting angry. I stood and met him eye to eye. "You've left viddy records of yourself all over the place. Anyone at all could have figured out who you are, and anyone with half a brain could have figured out you didn't die in that accident. It doesn't take a genius to put two and two together, Declan. Mecho technology is everywhere. Nobody talks about it because nobody wants to admit they're prejudiced, that's all."

"So what will it be?" He asked me, once again making me pause to think what he meant. "Money? I can get you that. Rank? I can help you there, too."

"You think I want a price to keep my mouth shut?" My throat burned with the sting of bile as I fought not to be ill.

"It's why you came here, isn't it?" He ran his hands through his hair again, giving me the cocky grin I hated and loved. "It's just too good to be true, right? Caldyx Adar isn't dead, he's mecho. What do you want?"

"I didn't come here to blackmail you." I kept my voice low to keep from screaming.

"Why did you come here, then, Gemma?" His voice went low, too. Smooth. Cruel.

His accusation clawed at me, and I couldn't tell him my reasons. Not now, after his accusation had clawed me to shreds.

"How can you think that?" I asked, even as I knew his answer could only wound me more.

"What else was I supposed to think?"

I shook my head. I refused to allow even one tear to slide down my cheek in front of him. His face blurred and I blinked rapidly to force away the tears. I kept my voice firm through force of will when I answered him.

"I think you want to be discovered. Living out as a mecho is better than living as a prisoner."

"What do you know about it?" His sneer did me in. I couldn't tell him anything, now.

I turned to leave. "Goodbye, Declan."

Two secbots greeted me as I stepped through the door. "Egress denied."

I had no patience for protocol. "Get out of my way."

Their pincer grips snapped down on my wrists. "Egress denied. Your presence is required."

"By who?" I demanded, wisely not struggling in their impossible-to-break grip.

Both bots replied in metallic unison: "Howard Adar."

*   *   *

I didn't tell Howard Adar to kiss my ass, though I dearly wanted to. Instead, I stared back at him as steadily as he stared at me. Watching him watch me made my palms moist. Howard Adar wasn't someone to mess with.

He sucked the liquid nicotine from the flexible rubber tube at the end of his holocig. Clouds of holo smoke wreathed his features, turning him into sort of a monster. He thought he was being imposing. I thought he was merely showing his true colors. Monster he seemed and monster he was.

"What sort of fool comes here, to my private abode, looking for my son?" He asked finally, and put the holocig aside.

"What sort of monster keeps his own son hidden away from everything just because he's different?" I'd said the word. Monster. If it offended him, he gave no sign.

"I've looked up your files, Gemma Ellen Trah. You of all people should know why Caldyx chose to remain in hiding."

I lifted my chin, unused to hearing my full name but not surprised he'd learned it. "Somehow I doubt he had much choice."

Howard lifted his hands in a mock-innocent gesture. "Every Newcitizen has a choice."

"He might as well have died in that accident, with the life you gave him."

"You speak of my son as though he were still a child." Howard took another swig of his holocig. "Yet I know you've experienced him as a man."

The thought of the man in front of me witnessing the lovemaking Declan and I had shared made me sick. "You had him followed."

Howard laughed, the sound merry and genuine. "Of course. You don't think I'd let him out there alone, do you? When what he is could cause such a scandal?"

"You *let* him return to the world." It became clear as Howard's face contorted in bemusement. "You allowed it, but you had him followed, to stop him if..."

"If he did something foolish?" Howard waved through the holosmoke. "Of course. Your profile didn't lie about you, Gemma. You're extremely smart. Tell me, sweet girl, were you always so brainy or did the computer chips the doctors slipped into your brain help you out a little bit?"

"I'm *not* ashamed of what I am." Even as I bit out the words, I knew he sensed the lie in them. "It's better than being dead."

"Not everyone would think so." Howard slipped his finger over the bottom of his cig to seal it and put it down in a metal holder on the table next to him. "Caldyx didn't."

"Then why allow him on the street at all?" I tossed the question at him, and he caught it neatly.

"Because I love my son, Gemma Trah. Because I couldn't stand to see him wasting away like he was."

"You could have sent him Offworld."

Howard made a tutting noise. "Offworld is for vacay or hard labor. Offworld is not for living. Not to mention that in the only suitable places to send him he'd have been almost instantly recognized."

"Why didn't you stop me from detaining him that night?"

He shrugged. "Why deny him some carnal pleasures? God-of-choice knows he hadn't partaken of any for quite some time. Not even the Pleasurebots I had especially ordered for him, and I can assure you I made certain he had the very best."

He paused to give me a smug look up and down my body that left me feeling as though I'd been dipped in slime. "Though I can see that not even the best bot can compare with your obvious talents."

He plainly didn't see the irony in his statement. My enhancements made me mecho, made me what I am. I could be despised or lauded for them, viewed with disgust or looked upon with lust. Yet despite the extra bits and pieces, I was the same person I'd been at birth.

"I'm good at my job."

"Care to show me how good?"

Apparently my look of disgust was enough reply for him. Howard's smile thinned and disappeared. Behind me, I sensed the sudden presence of the secbots. I tensed, knowing I couldn't run but ready to fight if I had to.

"If I'd known you were going to fall in love with him, I'd never have permitted you to fuck him in the first place," Howard told me.

The word love sounded dirty in his mouth. "It doesn't matter. He doesn't know I'm mecho too, and he thinks I can't stand to be with him because he is. He doesn't trust me, and he doesn't love me."

"No?" Howard's smirked insincerely. "Well, then. Tell me the amount to transfer to your credaccount, and you're free to leave."

"I don't want your money."

"No?" The smirk faded. "Someone who can't be bought can't be trusted to keep her mouth shut."

"Would it really be so terrible if everyone knew he was still alive?" My voice rose. "Why do you care what anybody thinks, anyway? You have enough money and power. Nobody would shun him, if only because he's your son! What difference would it make if the entire world knew he's mecho, Adar?"

"It would make a great deal of difference to his mother and his sisters," Howard replied. "And to me. And, I fear, to Caldyx himself. He's proud, as I am. You're absolutely right, Gemma. Nobody would shun him. At least not outwardly. But let's face facts. He is an Adar. He is my son. And, unfortunately, he is mecho. The relationships he would form, the friendships, might look past his disability because of his status and wealth. But Caldyx would know the truth, and it would eat away at him."

"Is it so impossible to think people would like him for the person he is rather than all of those things?"

Howard laughed in my face. "Really. I thought you were smart. Who in this world doesn't judge others by their status, their wealth and power? Who in this world could possibly love my son without having some consideration for who he is?"

"I did," I replied, and the secbots took me in their iron grips again.

CHAPTER 10

"It's imperative you keep your silence." Howard motioned for the secbots to drag me closer to him. "If money can't buy it, perhaps pain can."

The first blow caught me in the small of the back, just above my kidneys. I went to my knees, unable even to scream. Before I could even catch my breath, the next blow caught me in the stomach. I writhed on Howard Adar's priceless imported carpet, my fingers clutching the hand-woven fibers hard enough to break two of my fingernails.

"Impressive." Howard leaned forward to watch me squirm. "Not even a peep. Hit her harder."

One secbot whacked the side of my head with one of its metal paws. Bright spots flashed in my vision. A warm trickle I recognized as blood meandered down my forehead and into my eye, blinding me for a moment. The other secbot targeted my sides and back, raining a flurry of blows tightly targeted but no less powerful than its brother's.

"You could hire a VCTM for this and be better satisfied," I managed to gasp.

The next blow crunched my lips into my teeth. Blood gushed from my mouth, and I spit it onto the carpet. I curled into a ball to protect my head and stomach from the blows and tried to think through the pain.

They were metal. I am not, or at least most of me is not. They might not be able to break my metal bones, but they could do severe damage to my soft parts. Already the world was fuzzing out in grays and reds.

Somehow, I had to get to my feet and stay there, out of reach of Adar's secbots. Or else take the beating until he called them off. I didn't think he meant to kill me...but then again, I just wasn't sure.

I found some inner reserve of strength and rolled to my feet in a move that would have made Britney proud. Putting all my concentration into the leap, I forced my body to jump over the secbots' heads until I landed behind them. As I mentioned, they're strong, not smart. Without me in front of them to continue beating, the bots just stopped, waiting for command.

I was just glad he used metal instead of flesh security. Secbots can't be made smart enough to do anything but follow specific orders. Intelligence leads to decision choices. People are used for real security because there's nothing deadlier than a person who has the ability to choose, and still makes the choice of violence.

Howard looked pained. "Behind you, dolts!"

The secbots lumbered around to face me. I'd backed up against the door, fists raised to fend them off, though against the two of them the best I could hope to do was avoid them. My legs ached, because despite my extra hardware, I don't usually perform acrobatics like that. The blood flowed more heavily from my forehead from my efforts, and I swiped at it with my sleeve.

"Feisty." Howard shrugged. "You're not doing yourself any favors. Take the beating and prove you won't tell the world what you know about my son."

"I won't tell anyone, Adar. And not because of your money or your thugbots, either."

"Honor?" He sneered. "Oh, wait. Love. We'll see how long that lasts when you're still living in that hole of an apartment, fucking Pleasurebots to earn your wage. What will happen then?"

"It won't matter."

"I think you know as well as anyone how love can turn so quickly to hate." Howard sucked on his holocig. "But I see that pain is not a sufficient deterrent. How about this?"

He leaned forward to get a better look at me from around his bots. "I control Newcity. And if you cross me, you'll find out exactly what that means. Keep your mouth shut and stay away from my son."

I thought I knew already what his control meant, and as for staying away from Declan, he didn't have to worry about that either. "I told you already, Adar. He doesn't want to see me. He thinks I...."

"I know very well what he thinks. I know what was on that

holonote. Do you think he'd have been so upset, so unforgiving, without it? He knows your job is unpredictable."

"You sent the holonote?" I swiped again at the blood but no longer worried about his secbots. They stood like lumps of menacing metal, unmoving. "What did it say?"

Howard waved his hand, unconcerned. "Something about wanting to be with a real man. Something like that."

"Why? Why hurt your son like that?"

"There's no way on this gray earth I'd allow my son, my heir, to mate with the likes of a normal born citizen, much less a mecho. He was born for better things, or to be alone." He jerked his head toward the bots. "Take her out of here."

*   *   *

A night in the warm and healing waters of my bed left me revived, if not refreshed. With stiffness in every limb I forced myself to strip off the dreamcream and hobble to the bathroom. What I saw in the mirror made me wince.

I'd taken plenty of beatings since beginning my career with R.I.O. My time serving in the Oldcity Riots had even landed me a few days of sick leave to recover from my injuries. But those had been wounds requiring repair my body was incapable of completing on its own—what I looked at now was something completely different. Bruises covered my skin, most dark blue and black, some already edging their way to yellowish green. Marks of the secbots' fists stood out clearly in a few places, one on my belly and another on my left thigh. The rest of the bruises blended and covered each other, turning my skin into a crazy quilt.

My face was in even worse shape. Bruises masked my eyes, and my mouth had swollen around the cut left by one of the secbot's blows. I could only imagine how I'd have looked without the enhancements which allowed me to heal faster.

Hearing Kaelyn stir in her closet, I bent as quickly as my stiff muscles would allow and pulled a medkit from the cabinet beneath my sink. I didn't want her to see me like this. She'd been asleep last night when I'd finally made it home.

I squeezed a length of antiseptic blood thinner from its tube and smeared it over my face. It stung my eyes and smelled nauseating, but it immediately began working. The cream penetrated my pores and got to work on the bruises around my eyes, thinning the clotted blood and allowing my enhanced circulatory and lymphatic systems to remove them. It wasn't pretty and it hurt like hell, but it was a lot quicker than waiting for the bruises to go away on their own. The way the cream frothed slightly on application told me I'd been brewing the start of an infection, too, but that was also taken care of.

I couldn't do much to hide the cut on my mouth, but a quickfreeze pack helped the swelling go down enough to at least make me look somewhat normal. After five minutes, my face had drastically improved. My small tube didn't have nearly enough contents to take care of my body.

My monthly application of cosmetics should have lasted another week, but there was nothing left after losing the bruises. I flipped open the small key panel next to my mirror and punched in my keycode.

"Access denied."

I flexed my fingers, thinking the stiffness had made me fumble the numbers.

"Access denied."

Something was wrong. I tried again, but without much hope.

"Voice control on."

"Enter command."

"Explain denial of access for user GMMA 03271971."

System sounded tinny and harsh coming from the bathroom's small speaker. "Command override instigated."

"Origin of command?"

"Request denied."

I didn't need System to tell me, anyway. I knew who was behind this. Howard Adar.

In the bedroom, I pulled on a uniform and slipped into my boots. I slicked my hair back into a tight tail at the back of my head and pulled my cap low over my eyes.

Anger burned my gut, and I shook my head at Kaelyn's offer of breakfast. "Not today. I've got to get in to work."

"My Gemma was out very late last night."

I looked at her face, scrunched in concern, and paused to put a kiss on her fair silken hair. "I'm okay, Kaelyn."

"Will my Gemma be late tonight?"

I squeezed her close to me, feeling the rise and fall of her wings beneath my fingers. "I hope not."

She nodded, her hair brushing my cheek. "I will make you something special."

"You already have, Kaelyn," I told her as I let her go.

110

*   *   *

More trouble appeared when I clocked in at work. The retscan blinked twice, and System said: "Rescan necessary."

I'd already turned away, but at the order I went back. I lifted my chin to allow the retscan unobstructed access to my eyes. The red light flickered, checking.

"Citizen GMMA 03271971 report to Captain Rando's office immediately."

Being called in to Rando's office first thing in the morning was never good. Being addressed as Citizen instead of Officer was worse.

Rando was waiting for me, her face implacable as she waved me to a seat. "I'm sure you're wondering what's going one. I won't keep you in suspense. As of this morning, your position as Senior Op has been revoked. You are hereby operating under probationary status, as a Junior Op. If, at the end of the 90 day retraining period, you have proven yourself, you'll be removed from probation. Your status, however, will not revert to Senior status until you've re-met all the standards for that classification."

She was, in essence, demoting me. Years of work, lost. I'd expected something bad, but now her words so stunned me I could only sit, staring in silence.

Rando sighed. "Gemma, I didn't want to do this...."

"I know. You had no choice."

Her mouth thinned. "Did you think I really wouldn't discover that IIP mistake a few weeks ago? That, on top of the other incidents you haven't reported..."

There had been no other incidents, of course, but she'd been convinced otherwise. I nodded curtly, cutting her off without saying a word. "I know what's going on, Captain."

"Do you?"

Rando got up and floated in her chair to her door, shutting it with a click. She leaned against it to stare at me, her features crinkling with concern. "Gemma, what the hell is going on? You've been one of my top Ops since the day you started! I can't believe you'd have this many unreported incidents, but when I got the information from Internal Affairs, I had no choice. Who'd you piss off?"

I only shook my head, unable to tell her without compromising Declan. Rando sighed.

"Why'd you do it, Gemma? If you'd filed the report, I'd have recommended some refresher training. You're a good officer."

Would she have understood my reasons? That I had been protecting a man I now knew needed no protection, because he hadn't feared repercussion for his crime? My mistake had been in letting my heart rule my head, not in misidentifying him.

"Thank you," was all I said instead.

She shook her head at me again. "I didn't want to do this."

"I understand."

She went back to her desk and pulled her keyboard closer to her. With her attention focused on her viddy screen while she typed up a report, she dismissed me. I didn't bother to say goodbye.

When you're used to a certain standard of living, being demoted can be a real shock. Newcity operates on a complicated but precise system of plus and minus, with everything about a person's life contributing to their ranking in the city. Career, marital status, friendships, children, even the minutiae of training courses and inheritances factored in. Every citizen was ranked, constantly, up or down. Most people did little more than maintain their status, though there were always those who fought and struggled to rise in the numbers. In reality, your ranking number pretty much stayed the same your whole life. You might raise or drop by a couple of hundred, depending on who you marry or what training you take, but overall, where you're born is where you stay.

Those are privileges of position, not of power, and after my accident I'd tasted the latter. I'd become a Class A Citizen, with the added privilege of access codes and permission to use them necessary to perform my job. As I'd excelled in my career, my ranking had changed in subtle ways.

I could order groceries and supplies from home to be shipped regularly, and the amount deducted automatically from my credaccount, instead of having to manually place the order and wait for approval before shipment. I could obtain items commonly considered difficult or impossible to get, like Offworld fabrics. I could access illegal viddy programs, like political discussions and rallies in Oldcity. Things kept from the common people because Newcity operates on a "need to know" basis, and the average citizen just doesn't need to know.

Not any more. My demotion showed itself immediately when I returned to my cubicle. My viddy screen flashed the small flower icon I'd chosen to represent Kaelyn. A message.

Concerned, because she never called me at work, I accessed my personal account. System took a seeming eternity to boot up for me. I half-expected to hear the grinding of gears and see smoke rising from my cubby unit.

"My Gemma?"

Kaelyn's rosy face appeared on the screen.

"What's wrong, Kaelyn?"

"I tried to order dinner for tonight, and was denied access."

"Shitpissdamnfucktits." The curse ran together out of my mouth in a long string of anger. "I'll have to do it, K. I've…had some trouble at work."

She looked alarmed. "Is my Gemma ok?"

Guilt stabbed me at all I'd put her through these past few days. "I'm fine. But I'll have to go back to manual order for awhile."

She'd never been with me in a time when something she wanted hadn't immediately appeared. I could see her struggle with the concept. "I shouldn't order dinner?"

"Use what we have in the pantry, ok?"

She nodded, face solemn. I could see the disturbed flutter of her wings behind her. "You'll be home for dinner?"

I thought of Rando's ominous words, and recalled my brief training time as a rookie Op. I'd advanced so swiftly I'd barely had to suffer the indignities considered part of the experience, but I had no doubt I'd be in for it now.

"I don't think so. I think I'm going to be working a lot of extra shifts for the next few weeks."

The viddy screen beeped at me. "Personal communication limits initiated. You have two minutes to complete your communication."

"K, I have to go."

"I will make my Gemma something special," Kaelyn said. Her smile warmed me, if nothing else did. "And it will be waiting when you come home—"

Without further warning, the screen went back to its screen saver of shifting colors. I looked in the upper right hand corner at my personal settings and forced out another low curse. There were red Xs through nearly all the boxes. Personal communication had been set to a five minute limit, fifteen minutes daily max. Personal access codes had been completely removed, meaning I had to get approval from a superior before even keying anything in for research. The clock icon which showed my time left on the job blinked with no limit.

"Great." I had no quitting time. I needed superior permission for even that. "I wonder if I have to get a written permission to use the bathroom."

"Ask me real nice and I might consider it." Eddie slid into the seat next to mine. "Who'd you piss off, G?"

I sent a silent prayer to my God-of-choice. "Rando named you my immediate superior?"

"Yep." Eddie tilted back in the chair to stretch his long legs out on the desk. "Which means you have to do what I say. When I say it."

I gave him a look to show me that I wasn't amused. "This isn't funny, Eddie."

"Hell no, it isn't." Eddie shook his head. "All this from one IIP? I told Rando losing the runner wasn't your fault. She wrote me up for it, G, but she didn't demote me. What the hell is going on?"

I stared at him for a long time before I could answer. "I can't talk about it here."

He ran across his mouth and stared back at me. "You're in deep, whatever it is."

I nodded. "Don't we have some patrolling to do?"

Eddie didn't insult me by treating me like the junior Op I'd suddenly become. "We're assigned District 5 today."

"That's my fault, too, isn't it?"

He grinned. "Well, since prior to your little mishap I'd been working the upper class Districts and not the slums, I'd say it doesn't seem to be coincidence?"

I thought about putting my face in my hands but didn't. This wasn't going to break me. "I'm sorry."

Eddie shrugged. "Hey, it might be fun."

I cocked an eyebrow at him. District 5 is home to the lowest class bots and the citizens they serviced. This wasn't about fetish practice, or things outside the normal realm. This was about filth, and poverty, and crime. As close to real crime as anything in Newcity got. Drug abuse that went way beyond recreational. Illegal weapons. Eddie and I were not in for a fun time.

My stint in Oldcity had taught me poverty there was the rule, not the exception. Citizens didn't get ranked—there was no point. They didn't work. The relationships they formed and broke, and the children they bore were not part of any recognized marriage or bonding ceremony. Residents of Oldcity survived on the government issued ration packages containing food, beverage and the drugs which kept them satisfied with their lot in life.

Obviously the drugs often failed at their purpose, because Oldcity rocked with riots and crime.

Yet despite all that, Oldcity has a way of living, a standard if you will. An alien culture, shocking to the average Newcitizen, raised in comfort and cleanliness, and peace. Still, there were rules, enforced by habit and tradition in addition to the daunting presence of Ops who here and only here were allowed to carry weapons.

By contrast, District 2 is part of Newcity. Its only boundaries are the regular District boundaries, not the chemical barriers that break Oldcity and Newcity apart like conjoined twins under the surgeon's knife. District 2 is not forbidden to any Newcitizen—but only those with a purpose for being there ever visit.

Legalizing drugs 250 years before had effectively put drug profits in the pockets of the government instead of the dealers. Pharmaceuticals are a more common indulgence than candy, which by comparison doesn't fulfill the same need as completely. Those who can't control their addictions overdose and rid society of their undesirable presence without the effort and legality which used to be required, and those for whom drugs don't ruin their lives can indulge themselves for fewer credits than it costs to buy a viddy newscast.

What goes on District 2, then, is not precisely illegal, but instead foolish and very dangerous. Government regulated recreational pharmaceuticals are clean and cheap. There's something for almost every taste, and for those who need something else, there's District 2.

"We've done our time there before, G. It's no big deal."

There are a lot of reasons why I love Eddie, and this only reinforced them. "Why hasn't some hot chick snapped you up yet?"

He gave me a leer. "I'm still playing the field, baybee."

I reached out to touch a thread of silver planted in his blond hair. "Don't play it too much longer, Eddie. You'll going in for your first set of transplants the day after your honeymoon."

"You want to go to the bathroom or not?"

The thought of where we were assigned that day made me nod. "Hell, yeah. I'm not putting my butt down in any District 2 loo's."

"You have to learn to pee standing up."

"I already know how to do that," I retorted. "But I don't even want to stand in a District 2 lav."

"Let's hope we don't have to," Eddie said. "C'mon, let's go."

*   *   *

"Phew." Kaelyn wrinkled her nose. "My Gemma smells bad."

Her words were an understatement of grandiose proportions. I reeked. My day in District 2 hadn't gone well. Eddie'd flushed out a gaggle of illegally outfitted Pleasurebots, and they'd run us into an ambush. We'd been stink bombed.

That we hadn't been searching for the gang of bots and their leader, who made his profit from smuggling his illegal poisons inside their useful and active sex cavities, didn't matter. We found them, they fought back, we ended up choking and gagging on a dose of specialty stink.

"I'm going to take a long, hot shower," I told her. "And then I'm going to bed."

She wrung her small hands, and her wings fluttered in agitation. I could see she needed to tell me something but didn't want to, and I saved her the anxiety by asking her outright to tell me what she wanted.

"My Gemma must go to the market," Kaelyn whispered, shamefaced. "I could not order food today."

"Shit." I'd forgotten my demotion meant the daily deliveries had been canceled. Kaelyn couldn't go to the market herself. I had to do it.

"I'll go when I've cleaned up," I promised. "We can't have you starving."

She gave me a wan smile. "My Gemma would never let that happen."

So, even though the thought of heading back out to the street made me almost want to cry, I satisfied myself with a chemical spritz to rid myself of the stench inside of the luxurious hot shower I wanted.

I pulled on a casual outfit of tight fitting pants and shirt, both black. I slicked my violet streaked hair back beneath a dark cap, and didn't bother with refreshing my cosmetics.

I slipped the straps of my carrybag over my shoulders. This was only the second time I'd ever used it, but I was glad now I'd paid for the deluxe version. Filled with groceries and sundries, this bag would be heavy, and the padded straps and waist belt would help soften the load. "Make me a list," I told Kaelyn.

The list was simple, and small. It pained me to see it. She didn't ask for treats or luxuries, only the most basic of staples. Bread, protein substitute, vitamin supplements.

"Nothing sweet? No chocobars?"

She looked solemn. "I thought my Gemma might have more trouble. I didn't want to bother her."

"Chocobars are still on our approved list, Kaelyn." I hoped I was right. I wouldn't find out until I got to the distribution center. And if they weren't...I'd make sure to find some for her.

I hopped a pedtread and went the several blocks to my District's distribution center. I hadn't expected a line, and was unpleasantly surprised to find myself waiting in one. Apparently my District had a lot of folks who didn't rate high enough for auto delivery, or else there were very few but the powers-that-be made life ten times more difficult for them...just for fun.

Howard Adar's ears must have been ringing fiercely, because I cursed his name with every foul word I knew, in every language I could speak. I've downloaded the intergalactic translator software. I can speak a lot of languages.

Nobody made eye contact. It was a more shameful thing to be here than I'd realized. I kept my eyes down, too, as my cheeks burned with self-righteous indignation and I sent evil wishes Howard Adar's way.

When it was finally my turn I used the terminal touch pad to check off the things I wanted. Three out of five items buzzed obstinately when I tried to order them.

"Unavailable." System's cool voice informed me over and over. That I'd had them yesterday and the day before didn't seem to matter.

I left with my carrybag half empty. I'd been able to get the chocobars, but only by trading for them with a similarly belabored Newcitizen who was willing to part with the sweets to get some soap.

"What did you do?" He asked me curiously, with a sideways glance over his shoulder like he was afraid of being overheard. "I didn't pass my last competency exam."

"I didn't do anything," I told him curtly.

He nodded. "Sure."

I took the chocolate, gave him the soap, and ended the conversation.

Instead of taking the pedtread, I decided to walk. I needed to work out my anger and frustration, and the exercise would be good. Even with the carrybag's weight on my back, I was still hyped up enough to set off at a slow jog along the District's little used sidewalks. Careful not to stub my heavy boots on a buckled slab of pavement, I avoided the other citizen traffic as best I could.

Without planning my route, I ended up outside the gates of my District park. The one I'd met Declan that night not so long ago. Without thinking too hard about my reasons, I let the door retscan me, and when it opened, I went inside.

As usual, it was close to empty. The only inhabitants were an elderly man reading an old fashioned paper newspaper, a collector's edition probably. He shuffled the sheets at me as I went past him, back toward the gazebo and the fountain, and took a seat on one of the benches.

In times past, the old guy might have brought corn or seed to feed birds and squirrels. Now he simply sat and looked at his paper. When he'd finished, he folded it carefully and tucked it under his arm. With the dignity of someone who's not quite certain if his body will allow him to stand without falling, the man nodded stiffly at me and left the park. The silence he left behind was welcome.

I took off the carrybag and set it at my feet, then leaned back for a few moments. In this park, Declan and I had made love. It seemed as though I could still taste him on my tongue, still feel the whisper of his breath on my skin. All of it had been for nothing, and I didn't want to think about it.

Very quickly, I realized I had no choice. The ping of the door to the garden caught my attention, and I opened my eyes. In came Declan.

*   *   *

"What are you doing here?" My voice was cold, and it didn't shake. I was glad for that. I stiffened on the bench, then got to my feet when he began to come closer.

"I need to talk to you."

His tawny skin was pale, the lines around his mouth deep. He clenched his fists as he moved toward me, and my own went up in response.

Like unenhanced humans, I don't have much control over my body's instinctive reactions. Unlike them, however, I do have exaggerated responses. My body's flight or fright mechanism had been triggered by his aggressive stance, and unless he seriously backed off, I would do whatever I must to protect myself. I'd killed men who came at me with less animosity on their features.

I've said before that men aren't always swift on the uptake. Declan apparently didn't notice my stance or my expression. He kept coming at me with his hands outstretched and eyes and mouth grim.

I didn't want to believe he meant to hurt me, and I didn't want to hurt him, but my muscles tensed and I reacted. Just before he reached me, my leg lifted out from my hip and twisted. My foot missed his face by an inch—and it had taken an extreme effort to miss him.

My heart pounded, but I managed to spit out: "Don't come any closer."

He frowned, which actually made his mouth look softer instead of angrier. "Gemma, I don't blame you for being pissed…"

But he hadn't dropped his hands, and I was still in hyperdrive. He took one more step and this time, my foot didn't miss. It connected squarely with his jaw. Declan dropped like a stone.

With my foe felled, my body relaxed a bit. Instantly, I went to my knees beside him. The sight of blood on his mouth, blood I had put there, made me bite my own lip in response. I smoothed his hair back from his forehead, and the feeling of it under my fingers made my already clattering heart skip a beat.

He opened his eyes, and in the next moment, his hands were around my throat. The adrenaline rush which hadn't had time to fade returned in double strength. Inside, I knew I should have been more careful. Declan was a mecho too. His body would react as mine did, to protect itself. He didn't have my Op training and background, but he did have enhancements.

My mind knew this, but couldn't override my body, which now began fighting to protect itself. My hands grasped his wrists and tried to tear them from my throat, but Declan was a man, and mecho, and he had the advantage of superior muscle strength. My lungs expanded to better process the minimal air I was now bringing in. I straightened my legs and used the force of my weight to bring us both to our feet. With a swift, sweeping arm motion that had nothing to do with being mecho and everything to do with martial arts training, I disengaged from Declan by knocking his arms away from my throat.

At the sudden release of his hands from my throat, Declan stumbled back with an appalled cry. He held up his hands as if they were alien things.

"Gemma, I'm sorry! I didn't mean to hurt you!"

"I know." I regarded him warily. "Back off for a few minutes. Let us both calm down."

He turned his back on me and paced. He ran his hands through his hair. With the threat gone, my breathing slowed and my muscles no longer trembled with tension. I sat back on my bench and propped up my carrybag while I waited for him to talk to me again.

After what had happened between us, I should not have wanted to go to my knees before him, but I did. I shuddered and hid the motion by bending to push my carrybag against the bench.

When at last he faced me, he had the good sense to do it from a distance away. His posture still indicated tension, but he forcibly opened his fists to let his hands dangle at his sides.

"I didn't mean to scare you," he said.

"You didn't scare me." I took a deep breath. "It's an automatic reaction, based on signals you sent with your expression and your stance. My body registered you as a threat, and I got kicked into defensive mode."

"Because you're an Op." He narrowed his eyes to look at me, but in his gaze I caught a glimmer of comprehension. "It's your training, right?"

I stood and moved closer to him. I turned my head to show him the thin, nearly invisible scar snaking down my neck and across my chest. "I was in a very bad hoverbike accident during vacay on Solaria eight years ago."

He stared at me without speaking for a long time. Neither of us moved. He was smart enough to figure things out. I didn't have to spell it out for him. I waited to see his reaction, and the thought he'd at least know my truth sent a bubble of relief to lift my heart.

"You're mecho." He didn't stumble on the word, or look embarrassed by it, and why should he? He shared the same stigma.

"They replaced 98 bones, my kidneys, my spleen and my spinal column. I have an enhanced circulatory and immune systems, and they put an internal hard drive partition in my brain."

"I don't understand."

"What is there to understand, Declan? I'm mecho. Same as you."

"Why did you send that holonote then?" He'd advanced on me again, a little, but when he saw me tense he backed off.

I sighed, frustrated. "I didn't. I told you I didn't. I was late because of work. That's all."

"And I was so sure you wouldn't want to be with me if you knew the truth, I was ready to believe the note without question." He punched his fist into his palm. "I'm an idiot!"

I didn't want to be the one to tell him his father had been interfering with his life. I didn't have to. Declan, despite our misunderstandings, was smart.

"What happened to your face, Gemma?"

I touched my cheek, surprised. I'd forgotten about the bruises. No wonder the man I'd traded with in the distribution center had looked at me so strangely.

"I had a problem with some secbots."

"My father's secbots?"

I hesitated, then nodded. There was no point in lying about it. Declan swore.

I bent and gathered my carrybag. "I have to go. I shouldn't even be talking to you."

I meant to brush past him, but he reached out and grabbed my arm. His touch was soft enough not to trigger a response, unless you counted the way my heart trip trapped.

"I owe you an apology."

"You don't owe me anything." I felt my back as stiff as an iron rod, and I didn't turn to face him. "We fucked a couple times. It's not like we were in love."

My voice caught and broke on the last word like a glass dropped on the floor. I pulled out of his grasp and headed for the garden gate. His words stopped me.

"Gemma, I'm sorry."

"Me, too." But that couldn't change things between us, and I kept walking.

"Wait!"

I was almost to the gate, but I paused again anyway. This time, I turned. The weight of the carrybag dug into my fingers and I shrugged it around until it went over my shoulders again. Grief and anger warred within me, and anger won.

"Wait for what?" My voice was sharp and cold. "You made your feelings clear the other night."

"That was before I knew the truth about you."

I set my jaw and glared at him. "That I'm mecho too makes everything all right?"

He shook his head. "No, but—"

"You're right. It doesn't. You were so ready to believe the worst of me, you never even gave me a chance to explain myself. You ran away, knowing I wouldn't be able to find you! You didn't trust me enough to talk to me!"

"But you did find me," he replied, and gave me his damn cocky grin.

I wasn't going to fall for it. Not this time. "And I paid for that, believe me."

His gaze went to the fading bruises on my face. "I never meant for that to happen."

"But it did. And there's more, Declan. I was demoted in my job. I lost rank. I've lost delivery privileges and God-of-choice only knows what else I haven't discovered yet, because your father wants to scare me into keeping my mouth shut! I guess I'm just lucky he didn't have me killed!" I jabbed a finger in his direction. "And for what? Nothing! I thought we might have something together, but I was wrong. You don't care about me. You couldn't possibly, or else you wouldn't have believed I could have written that note."

"My father again."

"Who else but the great and mighty Howard Adar has so much to lose if the public discovers his only son and heir is mecho?" I spat to clear the foul taste of fury from my mouth. "Keep your apologies, Declan. They're worthless to me."

I turned again to go.

"Gemma, I have never felt about anyone the way I feel about you. I can't stop thinking about you. I don't want to be away from you any more."

He spoke quietly, without shouting, and so it was easy for me to pretend I hadn't heard. I kept going, pushed through the gate and came out onto the sidewalk. After the silence of the garden, the bustle and noise of the traffic outside seemed magnified tenfold. It hurt my head.

Anger welled inside me again. Easy enough for him to say, but not to mean. I thought of his face when I'd found him at the Adar complex, and of the cruel things he'd said. No. If Declan truly cared for me, he would have trusted me enough to tell me the truth about himself.

I stopped so suddenly several people on the pedtread turned their heads to stare. Trust. It was easy for me to accuse him of not trusting me, when I'd been just as guilty. I hadn't told him I was mecho.

"But I was going to," I muttered. Thankfully my voice didn't carry to the pedtread, or I'd have earned another few strange looks. "I was going there to tell him."

I held fast to the loose threads of my anger, but they slipped from my grasp and left me with nothing. He'd opened his heart to me, and I'd walked away. Now who was being unforgiving and distrusting?

Maybe he was still in the garden. I had to check. I'd just turned around to go back, when two huge forms loomed out of an alleyway and blocked my passage.

I hit the ground without even time to cry out, and then they were upon me.

CHAPTER 11

There was nothing subtle about Adar's goon-bots. They hammered me with metal fists and rammed me with the metal treads of their feet. The pain was so intense I couldn't even shame myself into silence. I covered my head with my hands to protect it. I couldn't afford scrambled brains. The rest of my body could withstand an awful lot of abuse, but not my head.

They'd had enough sense to pull me back far enough in the alley, so there was less chance of any Newcitizen coming to investigate the scuffling and the grunts. Though if anyone did come to see what was going on, I was sure that once they saw it wasn't a mènage but a beating, they'd disappear pretty fast.

The internal hard drive partition I'd told Declan about was worthless, most of the time. Now it allowed me to separate my mind from the pain being inflicted on me, so I could think. Secbots are big, and they're strong, but they're not smart. They rely on causing so much immediate and encompassing pain their victim is unable to respond. I had an advantage over them, and I was going to use it.

I curled into a ball, knees tucked to my chest, arms curled around my head, hands splayed over my arms. As I figured, they concentrated their blows on my back, trying to get my kidneys. I rolled over onto my knees so I was crouched on the dirty pavement. My cheek scraped the rough concrete. I waited for a pause in the beating, took my hands from my head, and pushed off from the ground. I straightened my knees and got to my feet in a smooth, fluid motion that belied my aches and pains.

At least they couldn't actually break most of my bones.

Without a pause, I kicked up and out. My foot hit the descending hand of one of the secbots, and it wobbled off balance. It didn't fall, saved by its solid treads. It knocked against the building behind us hard enough to scratch the plazbrick wall. The other secbot swung at me, but I ducked beneath the swing and kicked out again. This kick took out one of its glaring red optic beams. The secbot let out a muffled grinding sound of surprise and put its hands to its optic center.

Now the first bot came back for me. I flexed my fingers and jumped a little to loosen my bruised muscles. It swung at me, and I deflected its arm with a nifty little martial arts move that I learned from watching Britney's favorite movie. The Matrix might look dated now in terms of special effects, but it had some kick ass moves in it.

I can't hover in the air like Neo and Agent Smith, but I can jump high enough to kick the secbot squarely in the metal grill that served as its mouth. The heel of my boot bent and broke the grill, and the force of the kick knocked the secbot backwards. Its partner, weaving a little because of its vision problem, came back at me, and I kicked out its other eye. Even though I was sure Adar had paid for subsonic navigation and radar, blinding the bot would buy me a little time.

I landed from the kick with my feet spread apart and my hands raised. Both bots whirred and churned, chattering to each other in their private language of clicks and beeps. My guess was they were deciding what to do next, since I'd certainly surprised them.

What they did next surprised the hell out of me. Both of them slid their pincer grip hands into small openings that appeared in their torsos, and both pulled out identical silver cylinders. To any Newcitizen eye, they'd appear to be stunners similar to what I carried as part of my own uniform, but I knew better. These bots carried real weapons, the sort that have been illegal in Newcity for half a century. Laserguns, the kind that could kill.

Why should I have doubted that Howard Adar would consider himself above the law? I didn't recognize the type of weapons, but then I hadn't been Offworld in eight years. I didn't need to know the make or model to figure out pretty damn quick that they were going to make my aching and bruised flesh the least of my worries in about two seconds if I didn't react fast.

I ducked. The white hot glare of the laser hit the wall of the building behind me and scorched the plazbrick. The burn area was as large as my head.

They were quicker with their weapons than they'd been with their self-defense. The next shot came within seconds of the first. I avoided it, barely, by throwing myself to the side. I hit the concrete but didn't pause, just kept rolling. I rolled toward the secbots, aiming for their treads. The one whose optic center I'd destroyed aimed at me, but I rolled away as it shot. The laser struck its own tread and blasted the metal to bits. With a strangled roar, the secbot toppled over.

Its partner focused its red optic beams on me as I crouched at its feet. It didn't shoot. Instead, it reached down with its free hand and grabbed for me. It got lucky, and grabbed a handful of my hair. Its height allowed it to pull me right off my feet. I dangled only for a moment, then swung my legs until I hooked them over the secbot's shoulders. Its arm bent, and I bit my tongue to keep the scream of pain from my ravaged head inside.

The bot tried in vain to aim the laser at me in a way that wouldn't also injure itself. Weapons like that aren't made for close combat. I still had the advantage. I reached up and jerked my hair from the bot's grasp, and left a handful of violet strands behind. Using the strength of my stomach muscles, I held myself upright while still gripping the bot's shoulders with my legs. It twisted and turned on its treads, but it couldn't shake me off.

The downed bot didn't seem to have any qualms about making sure it hit only its intended target. It sent off a shot that skimmed my shoulder. The heat was enough to scorch my jumpsuit. The next shot came lower, and also missed me. It hit the other secbot square in the chest. The sizzle of scorching metal and stench of frying circuits were music and perfume to my senses. The bot twitched and jerked, and I lost my grip. I hit the pavement again, this time hard enough to knock the wind out of me.

I scrabbled at the concrete to get to my feet before the downed bot could re-aim. My luck had run out, though, because I found myself staring into the black end of the lasergun with no place to go.

"Terminate destruction sequence!"

The shout echoed through the alley. I didn't dare turn my head to see who it was, but I recognized the voice with no problem. The secbot holding the weapon pointed it further in my direction, using its radar to detect me since it couldn't use its visual circuits.

"Command number 1251999, terminate destruction sequence!"

The secbot didn't lower the weapon. "Termination command not recognized."

"Shit!" Declan came into view and stood between me and the bot. "Override previous command, override code 05161997, terminate destruction sequence!"

The bot lowered its weapon at last. "Command recognized. Awaiting further instructions."

He turned and held out a hand. I took it. I got to my feet, and we stared at each other for a long, long moment.

"I'm sorry, Gemma," he said at last.

I looked at the secbots which had very nearly just killed me. "Thank you."

He looked over at the metal thugs, too. "What do we do now?"

The bot with the broken tread managed to push itself upright. Its partner lifted its weapon. Both spoke simultaneously, though the one whose grill had been bent was incomprehensible. We heard the other one just fine.

"Instructions received. Termination sequence reactivated."

"Your father must have them on remote," I said as the secbot steadied the lasergun.

Declan stepped more firmly in front of me. "I'll take care of this."

"Target blocked by Newcitizen 10241960," said the bot with the weapon.

"Declan, that bot's aim isn't very good." I watched the other secbot trying to reach the weapon it had dropped when it fell to the ground. "I'd get out of the way."

"Instructions received. Termination sequence expanded to include Newcitizen 10241960."

To give him credit, Declan didn't sound surprised at the lengths to which his father was willing to go. "Let's get out of here!"

I crouched and leaped, and swiped the other lasergun off the pavement before the fallen secbot could reach it. The weapon's weight and controls were similar to a stunner, but different enough that my first shot went wild. My second didn't. The secbot on the ground fell back without another protest, its guts a smoking mess of burning wires.

Declan grabbed my shoulder and pulled me back as the remaining secbot fired at us. The blast winged Declan, singed his shirt and crisped the hair curling over his collar. We both ducked as the bot fired again. I whirled with the laser in my hand, and aimed for the secbot's face. They'd been given weapons to carry but not the shielding to protect them against their own weapons. It took me two shots, but I killed that bot, too.

We stared at each other in the smoke-stinking alley. The hand holding the laser trembled, and I let it fall to my side. Declan put his hands to my face hesitantly, his eyes searching mine for permission to continue. With the adrenaline no longer pumping through me, I felt weak and more than a little close to tears. I couldn't have resisted him even if I'd wanted to, and I didn't want to.

His mouth on mine pressed sweetly, then hungrily as I clutched at his shoulders and urged him on. It had been too long since we'd kissed, an eternity since we'd touched. I'd thought I'd never touch him again.

His hands found the tangled lengths of my torn hair and smoothed them away from my forehead. His eyelashes brushed my cheeks as he pressed kisses to my face and neck. When he put his arms around me to hold me closer to him, I let out a sighing moan at the combined pleasure and agony the embrace provided. With the immediate danger passed, my brain was no longer blocking the pain from my wounds. I didn't want him to let go of me, but I pushed him back, anyway.

"Give me a few hours, Declan. And maybe a handful of pain meds."

"Gemma, I'm—"

I put my finger to his mouth to shush the words. "Didn't I tell you I don't want your apologies?"

*   *   *

"We need to figure out what we're going to do."

Declan ran his hands through his hair. "My father is not a generous or kindhearted man."

"Really?" I touched the burn mark on his bare shoulder, then bent to kiss the spot.

A small sound from behind me made me turn. Kaelyn peered around the doorway, her eyes wide. Her wings fluttered so nervously her small feet barely skimmed the floor, a testimony to her nervousness.

Declan made a small sound of surprise. "Who's this?"

"Declan, this is my—" I broke off. I'd been about to say "my fairy," but Kaelyn was so much more than that. "This is my daughter, Kaelyn."

The smile on her face as she came to my side made me glad I'd caught myself. Declan looked at me with his eyebrow cocked. I put my arm around Kaelyn's delicate shoulders.

"Kaelyn, this is my friend, Declan."

She bobbed her head. The fluttering of her wings slowed, but only slightly. She didn't offer him her hand. "Hello."

"Hello, Kaelyn." Declan gave her a slightly milder version of the smile he'd wooed me with. It worked the same magic on Kaelyn, who blushed furiously and ducked her head against my side. "It's a pleasure to meet you."

I bent to look into Kaelyn's eyes. "K, I have to talk with Declan about some important things. Why don't you go watch the viddy for awhile?"

She nodded, noticeably less anxious to stun her brain than she usually was. I could see her curiosity about Declan, but I feared I didn't have time to do more than introduce them. We'd killed Adar's secbots. I didn't know what he'd do next, but I knew it wouldn't be good, for any of us.

I kissed her cheek and gave her a squeeze. "K, please."

She nodded again, her hair a fine, sweet smelling cloud against my face. Even her gentle embrace made me wince, and when she pulled away her face was pulled into a grimace of concern. "Is my Gemma all right?"

"I'll be fine, honey. Right now I need you to go watch viddy. Okay?"

"Okay." With a backward glance, she left the kitchen and went in front of the viddy.

"We don't have much time. Your father isn't going to let us get away with this."

Declan sighed and ran his hands through the mess of his hair again. I reached out, unable to help myself, and smoothed the spiky dark strands. "I know."

His face was bleak, and my heart went out to him. What would it be like, to have your own father reject you so completely? To try to have you killed because you might be an embarrassment to the family?

"My father died when I was a child," I said quietly as I slipped into the seat across from him. I took his hands with mine. "My mother died when I was twenty. Neither of them lived to see my accident."

"But if they had?" He asked. "Would they have turned you out?"

I squeezed his fingers. "I like to think not. But I don't really know. My husband did."

"You were married?"

I smiled at his growl. "Yes. For three years. It was Steve's idea to go to Solaria, and his idea to rent the hoverbikes. After the accident, he dissolved our marriage."

"Bastard."

In that moment, I loved him for his anger on my behalf. I kissed his hand and then laid it briefly against my cheek. "It was a long time ago."

"My mother stopped looking at me like I was her son. Her eyes just…slide past me as though I were a stranger. She's always perfectly polite, and perfectly cold. My sisters treat me as badly as they always did. But my father is the worst. He pretends nothing is different, nothing is wrong. When I told him I was ready to go back out into the world, he clapped me on the back and offered me a cigar. Like he was proud of me." Declan's face twisted and his hands bunched into fists beneath my fingers. "That son of a bitch. All along, he had me followed to be sure nobody found out who I really was. I'm not his son, I'm a liability."

"We need to get out of here, Declan."

He nodded. "I know. But where will we go?"

My stomach dropped at the thought of it, but I knew as I answered him we had only one choice. The word caught in my throat like barbed wire. I swallowed to keep myself from choking as I replied: "We have to go Offworld."

System's modulated voice startled us both. "Communication requested from Newcitizen 08111971."

"Eddie," I explained to Declan's curious expression. When his eyes narrowed, I continued the explanation. "My partner."

I crossed to the viddy screen and hit the acceptance code. "Eddie!"

Eddie's handsome face looked at me with worry stamped all over it. "G, what happened to you?"

"I've had some problems, Eddie. I need your help."

He didn't bother asking what trouble I was in. "Tell me what you need."

"We need to get Offworld, and fast. I've lost all my access codes, my credit account's been garnished, and I'm sure my passport's been put on restricted use."

Declan watched our interchange without speaking for a few minutes. Then he came and stood by my side. "I have money Offworld. It's separate from the Adar accounts. My father doesn't even know about it. If we can get Offworld, we can get to it. But I have nothing here."

Eddie thought for a moment. "You need to get to Oldcity. You can get everything there."

I nodded, refusing to think of Oldcity's dangers. "I have Kaelyn, Eddie. I can't leave her behind."

Eddie sighed. "I'll be there in twenty minutes."

"I know, Eddie." I grinned. "I love you, partner."

Declan tensed beside me as the viddy screen went black. "I thought you meant you worked with him."

I had to take a mental step back for a moment to register his comment. "Eddie is my partner. I do work with him. But he's also my friend."

"You tell all your friends you love them?" His dark eyes sparked, and his mouth turned down into a frown.

"Are you jealous?"

He allowed me to take his hand but didn't return the squeeze I gave his fingers. "Do I need to be?"

I shrugged. "Depends on you, Declan. Eddie and I have worked together for six years. Yes, we've been to bed together, in training and just for fun. But we haven't been lovers off the job for about three years now. Eddie has always been there for me, and I do love him. But..." I paused to clear the block in my throat. "But not the way I love you."

"Oh, Gemma." Declan enfolded me in his embrace. "I love you, too."

This time, I ignored the pain and let him hold me.

*   *   *

It was hard to explain to Kaelyn that we had to leave. Her small body shuddered in fear when I told her to choose only the most important items to take with us. I held her close, hating myself for having to do this to her.

I pushed her away so I could look in her face, but kept my hands on her shoulders. "Kaelyn, it will be all right. I'll take care of you."

"My Gemma will take care of me," she whispered, as though to herself. She looked around the bedroom, then at the small closet she'd always preferred to sleep in. "Take only the most important things?"

"Yes," I told her. I pointed to the small chest of drawers that held her robes and the few small items I'd bought her over the past year. "Pick the most important things."

Kaelyn put her arms around me again and squeezed. "My Gemma is my most important thing."

Tears filled my eyes at her words, and I squeezed her back. "I love you, K. I'm so glad I found you."

"I am so glad my Gemma bought me from that slave trader." She wriggled a little in my arms to get more comfortable. "Can I take my ronagh-beast?"

"Of course you can." I reached to the side and plucked the stuffed toy from the dresser drawer. "But we have to go quickly."

"Before the hunters come?"

Again, my heart ached at what she must have gone through. Kaelyn had been little more than an infant when the trader came through Keani and took her from her family. Only the tiniest Keanican could survive the trip and adapt to the change in gravity. She'd lived more than half her life in a cage before I'd bought her. Now I was subjecting her to more fear and upheaval.

"K, remember when I first brought you home, and you hid in the closet all the time?"

Kaelyn giggled. "I was afraid of my Gemma."

"But after awhile you started to come out, right? And you trusted me?"

"My Gemma was nice to me. You gave me chocobars. You gave me the ronagh-beast." She hugged the worn plush toy.

"You have to trust me now. I won't let anything hurt you. I promise you that, Kaelyn."

She hugged me again. "I will hurry."

I got up, my body making a million protests, and went back to the kitchen to Declan.

"Is that smart?" He asked.

"What?"

He moved his chin toward the bedroom. "Telling her you won't let anything happen to her. Where we're going...you can't really promise that."

"I can," I answered grimly. I looked toward the glimmer of fair hair in the bedroom. "I will die before I let something hurt her, Declan."

"You really think of her as your daughter, don't you?"

"She's the closest thing I'll ever have."

Silence fell between us. Neither of us would have children the normal way. I didn't know if Declan had ever thought of having children, but his citizen profile had shown he'd never had any.

"We'd better go," he said with a glance at the clock on the viddy screen. "It's been twenty minutes."

Less than an hour had passed since we'd busted Howard's secbots in the alley. I had the overwhelming sensation we'd wasted too much time. Information is instantaneous in Newcity. Howard knew the second his secbots went down.

I looked around the small apartment I'd lived in for the past eight years. Though I'd outfitted it with every luxury my Op salary and rank could provide, I couldn't pretend I'd be sorry to leave it. It was my dwelling, but not really my home.

Still, there were things in it that I didn't want to leave behind. Memories, good and bad, but part of my life. How to pack everything in the small amount of time and with the small amount of space?

I was saved from the dilemma by a knock at the door. Declan and I looked at each other, startled.

"My father," he whispered, though the door was three inches of plazsteel and nobody on the other side could possibly hear him.

I was inclined to agree. System hadn't beeped to warn us of any impending visitor—whoever it was had circumnavigated the building's front door code. Cautiously, I drew the weapon I'd stolen from Howard's secbot, and pointed it at the door.

The knock came again, a brief series of taps followed by silence and another set of taps. My muscles released all their tension, and I winced at the aches that followed. I heal fast, but I wasn't close to being fully healed yet.

"It's Eddie," I told Declan, and made for the door.

He stopped me. "How do you know?"

"The code." I had downloaded Evadian code and taught it to Eddie during one particularly slow shift early on in our partnership. We'd used it many times since. "It's Evadian."

He didn't let go of my arm. "My father would know that about you, Gemma. He can access your entire citizen profile, remember? He'd know you can understand Evadian, and that you communicate that way with Eddie."

I hesitated, but then reached up to touch his hand resting on my arm. "The only way to know is to open the door. If it's your dad's army out there—"

I stopped, aware of Kaelyn in the bedroom, packing her few belongings. My throat closed, but I continued. "We don't have much choice, D."

It was the first time I'd used the Newcity slang term of affection for him. He grinned and jerked his head toward the door, then took the hand not holding the weapon.

"Go get him, G."

I palmed the door open button and waited, weapon aimed. The door slid silently on its tracks, and revealed Eddie waiting outside. I lowered the weapon quickly, but the look on his face showed me he'd seen it.

His glance took in me, then Declan behind me. Eddie's blue eyes narrowed, and though he spoke to me, his words were meant for Declan.

"You're in a heap of shit, aren't you, G?"

"How'd you get up here without Gemma granting you access?" Declan came to stand by my side.

Between the two men, I felt the testosterone pulsing in the air. Under other circumstances, I might have been flattered, or amused. As it was, we didn't have time for a bunch of male posturing.

"Eddie has my personal access code," I told Declan. I looked to Eddie. "We don't have much time."

"I'm surprised you have any," Eddie said with another narrow glare at Declan. "Howard Adar doesn't like to be crossed. Or so I hear."

No matter what Howard had done to him, he was still Declan's father. My lover bristled. His hands bunched into fists. He didn't advance on Eddie, not quite, but if I hadn't been standing between them I can't guarantee that fists wouldn't have flown.

"Are you going to help us or not?" Declan asked. "Because if not, then get the hell out of here."

Eddie grinned, and shot me an approving glance. "He's got balls, at least. Guess he'd have to, to take you on."

Kaelyn's small voice interrupted the banter. "I'm ready to—Eddie!"

The small form nearly flew across the room to leap into Eddie's arms. Her wings fluttered, and she pressed her soft cheek to his with a sigh of rapture. Eddie, as always when presented with Kaelyn's exuberance, patted her back somewhat awkwardly between her wings and then set her down.

"I'm all ready to go," Kaelyn said.

"Visitors requesting access," System announced, and we all froze.

"Access denied." I spoke even as I ran to the bedroom to scoop up the small bag I'd managed to pack. Declan followed, close on my heels.

"Visitors requesting access," System repeated, its modulated tone now coming from the bedroom speaker.

"Access denied!" I shouted, but knew it was no use.

I tugged open the top drawer of my dresser so quickly it fell out. Personal items scattered everywhere, and I grabbed whatever I could lay my hands on. Kaelyn's purchase receipt, a holophoto cube...my wedding ring. Despite the urgency, I hesitated before tossing it in my backpack, but then did anyway. It was pure iridium, and could fetch a nice price in an Offworld market. We'd need the cash.

Eddie appeared in my bedroom doorway just as System spoke again.

"User command overridden. Visitors granted access. Level One."

"At least we have a warning," Eddie quipped.

Nobody took the time to smile. "We'll have to exit through the roof," I said.

"Unless they have guards up there already," Declan said grimly. He took the pack from me and slung it over his shoulder.

"Keep your fingers crossed," I replied. We had no other choice.

"Level Two. Level Three. Level Four."

I lived on Level 28. "Let's move it, now!"

Eddie grabbed up Kaelyn and her small bag. I followed with the bag I'd packed in the kitchen, and Declan came after me with my backpack. Instead of turning right to go down the hall toward the elevators, we went left, toward the stairs. Eddie banged open the door to the echoing metal stairwell, and we started climbing.

I was closer to the top than the bottom, which was a blessing. We paused before bursting onto the rooftop, and listened for the sound of metal tread feet on the stairs behind us. So far, nothing, but we still had no time.

Eddie eased open the roof door. Night had fallen since my encounter in the alley, and the bright neon lights of the District Lovehuts cast their glow into the sky. Nothing waited for us on the roof.

"My father is a cocky bastard," Declan said by way of explanation. He gave Eddie a grudging grin. "He doesn't expect opposition because he never gets it."

"Good for us." I pointed to the closest neon sign, just one roof over from ours. "We can cross the roof and get into that 'hut there. And then…"

"I'll take it from there," Eddie replied. "We'll do the Whitney maneuver."

"The what?" Declan asked.

Eddie shifted Kaelyn in his grasp. "About forty years ago, some Oldcity gangsters decided they were going to market unregistered intoxicants to the underground clubs. Without paying the registration fee to the Newcity governing body—"

"Including my grandfather." Declan nodded.

"Yeah. Well, without paying the fee, the gangsters stood to make a hefty profit. The problem was how to get the goods in and out of the clubs."

"They used Pleasurebots as carriers," Declan said, as though suddenly recalling. "Which is why so many of the regulatory inspection laws were passed."

"Exactly," I said. "They mostly used the LUV models, because they had extra storage capacity, but they used a number of the PSSN's, too."

"Whitney Scott was the leader of the group," Eddie continued. "Newcity Council knew it. But in order to arrest her, they had to catch her. They tracked her and a shipment to one of the 'huts, and waited until she came out."

"But she never came out," Declan said.

"She came out, all right," I answered. "But she looked and acted like a Pleasurebot. The secbots were programmed to read her citizen profile in her scan when she passed, but because she looked like a bot, she slipped past them."

"The Whitney maneuver." Declan nodded.

"Modified," Eddie said. He turned to the sound of metal-tinged voices coming closer. "They're here."

Kaelyn whimpered, and I took a minute to reach out and touch her fall of bright hair. "We'll be out of here in a few minutes, K. Don't worry."

She put on a brave face. "My Gemma won't let the hunters get me."

"Not ever again," I said.

"We promise," Declan added, and squeezed my shoulder.

*   *   *

Getting across the roof was easy, since the buildings weren't separated by more than a couple of feet. Even Eddie, who had just the standard law enforcement enhancements, could make the jump. Kaelyn made a startled squawk when we sailed over the space, but in seconds we were over.

"Your father really is an arrogant bastard," I told Declan as we entered the Lovehut through a rooftop access door and made our way down the levels of exuberant and abundant sexual activity. "He doesn't expect us to get away, does he?"

"If he did, he'd have more guards chasing us." Declan elbowed past a group of hopeful orgiasts waiting to get into a room. "I told you, he doesn't expect opposition."

The lack of stronger pursuit unsettled me, but I tried to think of it positively. Adar's arrogance could only benefit us.

The four of us left the Lovehut at street level and hopped the pedtread without a backward glance. If Adar's secbots had figured out our path, they were being remarkably discreet about following it. Or so I thought, until the pedtread slowed, then stopped with a slight jerk.

System spoke with neutral calmness from the row of speakers set into the buildings across from us. "All Newcitizens prepare for random retscan in accordance with statue 1241624. Repeat. All Newcitizens prepare for retscan in accordance with statute 1241624."

"Census update," Eddie muttered. "Clever."

As much as people didn't like being stopped on their way to debauchery and decadence, the grumbling was minor. Taking census was a common, if annoying, part of regular life in Newcity. Without it, the marketers would have no idea just what brand of toothpaste to tempt you with, or what color thong you might prefer. People have grown so used to their personal preferences being recorded; I'm not really sure what we'd do if we had to actually remember them for ourselves.

Behind us, the crowd on the pedtread had obediently, one by one, stepped up to the retscan units, blinked against the red beam, and returned to their spots.

"Does he think we're idiots?" I said aloud as we stepped off the pedtread. "That we'll just step up to the retscan and let ourselves be found?"

"Why not?" Declan asked. "They did."

He was right, of course, and not for the first time I wondered about giving so much power to one family. But then, I thought, as I followed the man I'd fallen in love with, we hadn't given the power to the Adar family. They'd just taken it.

It appeared Howard Adar had more than just his secbots looking for us. From the line of hovercraft in the street came ten or a dozen blue-uniformed Ops from. With a sinking heart, I recognized several from my unit.

"RBRTA 12381965 and TMMY 19601238." Eddie muttered. Kaelyn shifted in his arms, and he set her down.

She clung to my legs, and I realized how terrified she must be. She hadn't been outside since I'd bought her from the slave trader. Now, among the crush of people and fleeing for our lives, I was amazed she wasn't sobbing. I gave her a quick squeeze to reassure her, but her shoulders still trembled. Her wings bunched the back of her light cloak, making her appear hunchbacked.

It's not the Recreational Intercourse Operatives' job to take census, and I heard more than one surprised exclamation as the officers mounted the pedtread in search of us.

One reason Eddie and I are such good partners is our ability to guess what the other is thinking. Without saying anything, we each moved to one side of Declan, and took his arm. That meant I had to let go of Kaelyn, but I could still feel her behind me.

"Make way," Eddie said to the crowd. "Prisoner escort coming through."

The crowd parted, more surprised murmurs following us as we pushed through the crowd away from the other officers.

We headed for a stopped hovertaxi across the street. Behind us, the shouts started. Eddie and I picked up the pace.

"Where to….ahh, it's you!"

I don't believe much in coincidence, which means fate had planned for the driver of this taxi to be the same Dieselian who'd helped me twice before.

"Are you the only hovertaxi driver in Newcity?" I asked as we all slid into the back seat.

He shot me a grin that made his scarred face handsome for a moment. "For you, pretty lady, I think so."

"We need to get to Oldcity," Eddie said.

The Dieselian shook his head but started the craft. I clutched Declan's hand as it rose into the air. Kaelyn whimpered on my lap, but then peeked out through the window in interest as we took off.

"You got company," the driver said nonchalantly as the first Op hovercraft rose behind us.

"Outrun him," Eddie said.

"Man, you just made my day."

True to his word, the Dieselian pulled the accelerator lever all the way. We shot forward, nearly rear-ended a slower moving craft in front of us, then bounced up another five feet to avoid the crash. My stomach lurched to my throat and my fingers made red impressions in Declan's hand. I closed my eyes.

"It's all right, my Gemma," Kaelyn whispered in my ear. I felt the soft touch of her cheek against mine. "We'll be all right."

I had to take courage from this child, if I could not take it from myself. I forced my eyes open. "Holy God-of-choice!"

The Dieselian had popped the hovertaxi up another twenty feet, and now zoomed not just faster than the other traffic, but above it.

"It's illegal to hover more than ten feet above street level!" I cried, the words sounding foolish even as I yelled them.

The Dieselian laughed and shook his shaved head. "You want to get to Oldcity, you got six hovercraft full of bluesuits behind us, and you care if I'm breaking traffic laws?"

"She doesn't like to fly." Eddie leaned across Declan to pat my shoulder. "She'll be okay. Won't you, G?"

I couldn't answer, because at that moment the taxi jerked to the left to head down an alley—the wrong way. In a second, I saw why. We were being chased by not only the R.I. Ops, but also the regular traffic enforcers. Their distinctive yellow and red vehicles fell into line behind us, followed by the blue R.I.O. cruisers.

"Who'd you piss off so bad?" asked the driver.

"My dad." Declan gave a short laugh.

The Dieselian returned the chuckle. "What'd you do, stay out after curfew?"

"Something like that." Declan slipped his arm around my shoulders and continued to allow me to squeeze his hand nearly blue.

I didn't think we'd get out of it, I really didn't. Not with eight hovercruisers behind us and more alerted to our direction. It had been a valiant effort, and my one regret was that I'd involved Eddie and Kaelyn in my adventure.

Never underestimate a Dieselian. They are a race of daredevils, adventurers and escape artists. Our driver pushed his rattling hovertaxi to its limits, and he left our pursuers behind like they weren't even there. I'm not proud to say Newcity law enforcement is much like Howard Adar—not used to being opposed. Peace has its pros and cons. At least it worked in our favor.

He couldn't take us all the way to Oldcity, of course. Hovertraffic can't operate outside the dome and its slightly lesser gravity. He took us as far as District 100, though, and refused the credit account number Eddie gave him.

"Nah," the driver said with a slow grin in my direction. "If you get caught for this deal they'll just take it away from me. I'll take something else."

"Listen, jerk—" Declan began, but the bigger man just held up his hands to stop him.

"Not that, man." The Dieselian looked at me. "I can see she's your lady. But I'll take a kiss."

Declan didn't like that, either, but we owed the driver something, and his price wasn't really that high. Besides, I'll admit to some curiosity. I'd never kissed a Dieselian before.

I'm not used to being made to feel small, but in front of this man, I did. His arms were the size of one of my thighs, his chest fully as muscled. His shaved head gleamed in the light shining from inside his hovertaxi.

He ran his fingers along the thin silver line of my scar and gave me a grin that could have made my knees weak...if Declan hadn't been glaring at me. His mouth was surprisingly soft, his lips firm against mine. I hadn't thought he'd press his luck, not with two men giving him the evil eye, but Dieselians aren't known to back down from anyone.

He took his time with the kiss, never asking too much and never taking more than I was willing to give. It seemed to last a minute and an eternity, his mouth on mine and my hands splayed against his massive chest. Who'd have thought kissing could be so tranquil in the midst of pursuit?

Eddie's voice broke me away from the embrace. "Damn, G. Quit with the tonsil hockey already and get your ass in gear!"

The Dieselian stepped away, large hands outspread in Declan's direction, to show he'd meant no harm. I felt a little dreamy, a little woozy, and realized he was laughing at me.

"Think about that, pretty lady," he said. "When you're heading for the stars. Maybe it'll help you."

I didn't have time to ponder what he said, because in the distance we heard the droning wail of sirens.

CHAPTER 12

Declan and Eddie had the two small bags I'd brought. I grabbed Kaelyn. She pressed her face into my shoulder, hard enough to hurt against my recent wounds, but I didn't tell her to stop. Fear made her cling to me, and me to her.

Suddenly, I was terrified in a way I'd never been facing even the most frightening situations. I feared losing this inhuman creature I'd come to love as my own child. I feared losing the man I had taken as my lover after so many years alone. I feared losing one of the best friends I'd ever had.

Sheer terror can motivate a person to action, or freeze them solid. I clutched my child, felt the softness of her hair against my face, and thought it would be the last sensation I would ever have. Then my eyes opened, as though someone had tugged the lids, and my gaze met Declan's. He didn't pull at me, or yell. He only nodded, once, slowly, as though he'd seen directly inside me and discovered the secrets of my heart.

All at once, I had no trouble moving. With Kaelyn clinging to my neck, I reached with one hand for Declan and the other hand for Eddie. "Two blocks and we're home free, guys!"

That wasn't quite true, but close enough. We ran, and if we escaped Newcity because Howard Adar wasn't used to opposition, I'll forever count my blessings to that effect. We fled through the deserted streets and reached the city's edge. The line of demarcation is an amazing sight, even in the dark. To untrained eyes, Newcity simply…stops.

Eddie and knew differently, of course, as we'd been assigned terms of duty in Oldcity. We didn't hesitate, but ran toward the blank, faintly glimmering edge of the anti-UV dome which encloses Newcity from the elements. Declan was on my heels.

"Where's the door?" He cried.

Eddie swerved just before making contact with the barrier itself. We ran along its edge. This close, the chemical stench of it was enough to make Kaelyn cough and my eyes water.

"Zip," Eddie gasped out without stopping.

"What?"

I knew what he meant. The dome is constructed from manmade components that reflect the sun and keep the synthetic atmosphere intact inside Newcity. It is, however, impossible to keep the dome completely tied to the earth all the way around its perimeter—another engineering faux pas that had never been fixed. Most Newcitizens don't know that "real" air and sun sometimes make their way in through small slices in the dome called zips, unless they've had the misfortune to smell the air or feel the burn of the sun.

"A zip is a rip in the dome," I explained quickly, not for the first time glad for my enhanced lung capacity that allowed me to breathe and speak and run at the same time.

"I know what a zip is," Declan said. "I just didn't think you would."

Eddie made a disgusted sound in his throat. "Your pops can't keep everyone in the dark, Adar. Who do you think gets sent out when there's a complaint about the dome? Not just techs. Us Ops get sent out, too."

"Shut up and look for a zip," I snapped, not interested in listening to them spar anymore.

I shifted Kaelyn's weight. My aching arms weren't going to hold out much longer. Even with all the mecho functions, my body was wearing down. I needed rest, badly, to heal and repair.

"How do you know there's a zip along here anywhere?" Declan asked me.

"There's always zips," Eddie replied. "Ten years from now, the whole dome's going to come down on us."

"Make it more like five." Declan's voice was grim.

"Shit." Eddie paused in his jog to look more closely at the opalescent barrier. "Guess you know something us peons don't?"

"I think I found one!" I cried. I set Kaelyn down to step up to the dome's edge.

The barrier is only eighteen inches at its thickest point. Here, in this spot, the smooth surface was marred by a zigzag pattern of glittering specks. A small zip.

"Let me take her," Declan told me as I hunched down to let Kaelyn climb up on my back.

Her clutching fingers answered for me. "I've got her."

"If she's too heavy for you…"

I felt her tense against me, and knew I couldn't deny her the comfort touching me brought her. "I'm okay."

"Let's go." Eddie stepped up to the zip and put his hands against it. "Here goes nothing."

I followed him. Pain, brief but intense, seared my flesh as I breached the dome. My skin tingled from the dome's electrical and chemical makeup. It was only eighteen inches thick, but it felt like eighteen feet.

Then we burst through it, Kaelyn and I, and fell to the ground beyond. No smooth concrete here, no plazbrick paths. Ancient, buckled pavement tore my knees and hands as I caught myself before I crushed the girl who clung to me so tightly. Stenchful weeds, gray and hideous, grew in the cracks. The remains of a building, once taller than any Newcity skyscraper crumbled to our left, and to our right, an ancient pedtread loading station loomed out of the dark.

Few people resided this close to the dome wall. There was no benefit in it, and long term proximity caused nausea and headache from the chemicals needed to create the barrier. Several blocks away, lights burned.

"Glad we made it at night." Eddie rubbed his knees where he'd also scraped them on the jagged pavement. "Have you ever seen the sun?"

Declan brushed off his hands. Of all of us, he'd been the only one to keep his feet. "Earth sun? No."

Eddie made a face. "Let's hope you're out of here before it rises, then. You'll fry like an artiegg."

I wouldn't, and neither would Declan, because of our enhancements. Being mecho did have advantages. Eddie and Kaelyn, however, had no such protection. Their skin, unused to the UV rays the holodome protected Newcitizens against, would redden and blister without appropriate precautions.

I put Kaelyn down to stretch my back and shoulders. She was small and light, but still a burden after more than a few minutes. I worked at my tense muscles with my fingers, knowing I'd have to pick her up again.

She looked around curiously. "Where are we?"

"Oldcity, honey," I told her. "Hopefully we can find some people here who will help us get Offworld."

She looked doubtful. "This place stinks."

It did smell in a way Newcity, with its constant air circulation, didn't. "That's just…people, K."

She looked surprised. "My Gemma doesn't smell like that."

"I would if I didn't take a shower for a few weeks." I didn't mention the rampant disease Oldcitizens often suffered, either. Germs all Newcity residents, human or not, had been inoculated against bred and cultivated freely in Oldcity.

She wrinkled her nose. "Yuck!"

Eddie looked back at the dome barrier, which remained unbroken. "They might not know exactly where we went through, but they'll be sending Security Ops instead of R.I. Ops in here pretty soon. We have to find shelter, and passage out of here."

Eddie pulled a billed cap from his back pocket and put it on. His wallet, which came out with the cap, he left on the pavement.

"Guess I won't be needing that any more."

Declan made a rough sound in his throat. "When we get where we're going…"

Eddie turned to stare at him, his blue eyes questioning. "Yeah?"

Declan shrugged and held out his hand, which Eddie took. "I'll see you get back everything you had. And more. For helping us."

Eddie shook Declan's hand, and shot me a grin. "Hell, without G riding shotgun, I couldn't manage, anyway. Time to move on to brighter pastures. I've always wanted to move Offworld."

"Thanks, man." I could see how difficult it was for Declan to say such a thing, which made it mean all the more.

Men don't waste time with mushy sentiments, though, and that brief exchange signaled the end to their bonding. They each grabbed a bag, and I picked up Kaelyn again. We set off down the deserted, decrepit street, and sought a place to hide.

*   *   *

It wasn't as difficult as it would have been in Newcity. Oldcity is a haven of thieves, Earthen and Offworld-bred. There are plenty of places that'll offer succor to strangers—for the right price. Of course, the people who run them will turn their visitors over to their pursuers for another, higher offer, but for now at least, we had a place to stay.

Newcity credits are useless in Oldcity, which has no automated supply delivery, no viddy, not even any constant source of power. What luxuries the city had reveled in three hundred years ago had been dismantled or destroyed while its sister city grew and flourished with nothing more than eighteen inches to separate them.

"Not used to slumming, eh?" Fostruff, the grizzled man who'd taken the contents of our pockets in payment for a night's shelter pointed at Declan. "Not you, eh?"

"Food?" Eddie asked rudely. "We paid you enough, old man."

The man, who was probably only a few years older than me, lifted his hands and backed off. "Yeah, I'll get your food."

"Don't ask what it is," I told Declan under my breath. "Just…eat it."

He leaned over to whisper in my ear. "I'm not the naive prude you seem to think I am. I spent some time in Class A survival camps Offworld, Gemma."

"For fun?" I asked. "Good God-of-choice, why?"

"To prove something to myself." His answer was serious.

"And did you?"

He brushed his hands along my cheek. "Only that what I was trying to prove really wasn't that important."

"I'm sleepy." Kaelyn nudged her way onto my lap. This ordeal had made her far more affectionate and clingy than she'd been before, or perhaps it was the change in our relationship. I didn't mind.

I tucked the soft floss of her hair behind her slightly pointed ears and smoothed her jersey. "I think it's time you're in bed, then, don't you? We have a long trip ahead of us tomorrow."

She nodded, then yawned so hugely the sharp points of her teeth showed all in a row. I took her to the back room we'd rented and put her on the pallet. It was clean enough, at any rate, with no sign of vermin. We'd gone to a lot of hostels before settling on this one.

"Sweet dreams, Kiki." I pulled the covers up to her chin, and she closed her eyes. I kissed her forehead and took in the fresh scent of her for a few moments. Keanicans have a life span approximately twice that of humans, yet they reach maturity about twice as fast. Kaelyn wouldn't be a child much longer. What that meant for us, I couldn't know. I only knew that I loved her as much as I could ever have loved a child I could have carried in my womb.

With another kiss that made her smile in her sleep, I left her. By the time I returned to the front room, our host had provided several bowls of thick gravy and a platter of some brown sliced something or other that smelled suspiciously like artibeef.

"Don't ask, remember?" Declan told me as he stabbed a piece with a broken-tined fork.

The Adar family probably dined on meat several times a month, but real beef hasn't been available to the public for about one hundred years. Oldcity didn't get the shipments of algae processed into foodstuffs, and it certainly didn't raise cattle. I took my own advice—I didn't ask.

Whatever animal it had come from, the meat was surprisingly sweet and tender, with an undertang of wood smoke from being grilled. I had real beef once, just a taste, at Alfie Zoydman's house. He'd received a package as a gift, and he'd eaten it while taking one of his forever-long soaks in the tub. He'd let me taste just a bite.

Eddie returned from the hall with a piece of crumpled paper scribbled on both sides. He laid it flat on the table while he helped himself to a plate of food. He didn't even comment as he chewed, but Eddie would eat anything.

He pointed at the crude map on the paper. "We're here. Closest checkpoint is over here. We got lucky."

The zip we'd found was meters away from the closest official door through the barrier, which worked in our favor. "Still, it won't take them long."

"My father commands the entire Newcity Security system." Declan paused, swallowed, touched the map. "But I don't think he'll risk sending more troops than what followed us last night."

"No?" Eddie asked.

I shook my head, thinking of how much Howard Adar feared the public learning of his son's nasty secret. "Even he'd have to explain using such large amounts of force somehow. He won't want to draw undue attention to the chase."

"So a dozen officers, no more." Eddie chewed some more, swallowed. "What the hell is this stuff?"

"Don't ask," Declan and I said together, and we laughed.

The laughter lifted a weight I hadn't realized was on my shoulders. We weren't out of trouble yet, but being able to laugh made things seem much brighter. We had shelter, we had food, and for the moment, we had a chance at escape.

"Fostruff says he can get us in touch with a pair of Annvillian traders who're heading Offworld tomorrow." Eddie smoothed the paper to point at another location about 20 blocks from where we were. "Here. He says they'll be willing to take half payment now and the rest when we get to Annvilla."

"I can handle the amount when we get to Annvilla," Declan said. "But what are we going to do about now?"

"We'll figure it out." How, I didn't know, but with my belly full my mind's attention was turned to other things, like the pain in my muscles. "Didn't Fostruff say there was a bathroom around here?"

Eddie folded his map and put it in his pocket. "You go ahead. I'm going to get some shut eye. We need to leave just before first light."

Declan and I stared at each other across the table after Eddie went into the back room. It seemed foolish to be thinking what I was when this was not the time, nor the place, but the heart rules the mind, not the other way around.

"Come with me?" I asked, and held out my hand, and he took it with no hesitation.

"Anywhere," Declan said.

*   *   *

What Fostruff had called a bathroom was little more than a closet with dripping, stained sink, toilet and a narrow but deep plazglass bathtub standing on rusted metal legs above a glowing brazier. He had promised hot water, though, which was a luxury worth every cent we'd paid him, even if the water was synthetic and not real.

The tub was just wide enough to allow Declan and I to sit facing each other. The water came up to our chests, cloaking us in blessed heat kept at temperature by the glowing coals beneath.

I've experienced a lot of sensual pleasures in my life. They can't be avoided in Newcity. Enfolding myself into that hot water, though, allowing the heat to seep into my abused body, and sharing it with Declan, surpassed anything I'd ever encountered.

There are men who, sensitive to the ordeal we'd just shared, would allow a woman to simply soak in the water without expecting her to force her injured body to engage in intimacies. Thank my God-of-choice Declan is not a man like that. He put one hand on my shoulder and the other behind my head, and kissed me.

I sensed a heat in him that had nothing to do with the temperature of the water cradling us, and I thought of the Dieselian with a smile. Declan been jealous. My lips curved beneath his until he urged them open and swept the inside of my mouth with his tongue. Then I couldn't smile anymore.

My hands slid up to tangle in the thickness of his damp, dark hair. He pushed against me, the tub giving us little room to move. My back pressed against the smooth plazglass, and my legs parted to allow him closer to me. He moved between my thighs, his erection nudging my stomach, his chest scraping my breasts. He left my mouth long enough to murmur my name, then slanted his lips back across mine before I could reply.

I had to answer with my hands and my tongue, and by slipping my heels over the back of his bent legs to urge him closer to me. He responded, slid his hands from my neck and shoulders to my buttocks, and lifted me. He slid into me with no resistance, my legs hooked around his waist, my arms wrapped around his neck. And still we kissed, kissed, each breathing in the air the other let out, until we filled each other completely.

I came within seconds, and he took my moan inside his mouth and answered with one of his own. His finger curved around my rear, pulling me closer and sliding me back. I rode the crest of my climax and shuddered with it, then felt it rise again within me.

He twisted his hips against me, giving me that last bit of pressure, and I felt stars explode inside me again. He joined me this time, his buttocks clenching beneath the hand I slid down to clutch with. So sensitive had I become I felt every throb as he spent himself inside me.

He put his lips to mine softly one more, then rested his head against my shoulder. I smelled his hair and held him close. I didn't want to let go.

Arousal can make anyone forget the body's most stringent complaints, but after orgasm it's harder to ignore them. Declan and I separated, each going back to the small space the tub allowed us. I sunk into the water as far as I could. I couldn't stretch out, but the heat still felt good. I dozed a little, content for now in the afterglow of our lovemaking.

"I do love you, you know." His quiet words startled me into opening my eyes.

"We don't really know each other very well, D."

My answer didn't put him off. "Do you have to know someone to love them?"

I curled my arms around my knees to think for a minute. "I think it helps."

He tucked an escaped strand of my hair behind my ear. "What color is your hair, really?"

I fingered a section of violet. "Red."

"Red like a retscan beam or red like a Shaddran sunset?"

"I've never seen a Shaddran sunset."

He settled back in the water. "I have. It's beautiful. I'll bet your hair is that color."

"That's not exactly what I meant." I sighed. "Declan, my heart is telling me one thing, but my mind...."

"Don't listen to it," came his advice, coupled with a kiss that flushed my cheeks even more than the hot water had.

"Things might change between us," I ventured, hating the practical part of me that seemed determined to keep him at arm's length despite all we'd been through. "After this is over."

"Tell me about your childhood," Declan said as though I hadn't spoken. "And I'll tell you about mine. Tell me your favorite color, food, what books you like to read."

His questions made me smile. "What is this, twenty questions?"

"I want to know you, Gemma," came his reply. "So you won't have any reason to doubt that I love you."

Declan must have earned his strength of character on his own, but heredity had granted him his charisma. In that moment, it was clear who he was and where he'd come from, because I could have no doubt he meant what he said.

So we talked long into the night, until at last the fire burned out and the water turned cool, and then we crept back to our rooms and slept curled in each others arms.

* * *

The Annvillian traders turned out to be a husband and wife who owned a rust bucket spacecraft that looked like it would fall out of the sky before it could break atmosphere. My palms began to sweat at the sight of it, and my heart trip trapped in my chest. Kaelyn squeezed my hand, offering me as much comfort as she could.

The wife, a mousy, plump woman with a kind face, looked at Kaelyn with something like wonder. "She's pretty, ain't?" She asked in a thick, Annvillian accent. She reached to touch Kaelyn's silken hair, and Kaelyn shrunk away from the woman.

The husband of the team kept glancing nervously to the door of the warehouse they used as a hangar. "What you got for trade?"

We'd paid for Fustroff's hostel by digging in our pockets for items we thought might be worth something in an Offworld market. Simple luxuries like the chocobar Kaelyn had tucked into her bag were worth a lot more in Oldcity, but wouldn't be enough to get us Offworld.

"I have this." I showed him the iridium ring glittering in my palm. He reached for it, and I closed my fingers around the metal. "You get it when we're safely out of atmosphere."

He rubbed his hands together with another shifty glance at the door. "And the rest?"

Declan stepped forward. "When we get to Annvilla. 5,000 Intercolony Credits."

The wife still looked wistfully at Kaelyn. "My little girl had hair like that, wunst."

"Would you hesh up, woman?" The man snapped. He shrugged. "Our Becky got the Cleonan pox some years back. She died of it."

"I'm sorry." My compassion for the woman was marred by her husband's shifty manner and lack of sympathy to his wife's feelings. "When can we leave?"

He began to tick off a list on his fingers. "I have to load the bays awhile, and chart the course—"

Now the wife, perhaps sent over the edge by his casual dismissal of her pain, whirled to face him. "Whyn't you tell 'em the truth? You're gonna take their money and—"

"Shut up, woman!" The trader backhanded his wife to silence. A bright runner of blood trickled from the corner of her mouth, but she didn't even sob. Dry-eyed, she cast one last longing glance at Kaelyn, and then went up the ship's rickety pull down staircase to disappear inside the hull.

"Take our money and what?" Eddie's voice was cold.

The three of us presented a formidable sight, even for a trader who must have been used to far rougher company. He stepped back and passed his hand over his bearded chin. Another glance at the door had me turning to look, too.

The cost and risk of adding psi boosters, computer chips which gave the user telepathic, empathic or precognitive abilities, had kept me from adding such enhancements. Plain old woman's intuition ruled me now, and just before the door opened, I knew what I'd see.

"I'm disappointed in you, Caldyx. Didn't that time in the survival camp teach you anything? Never underestimate your enemy." Howard Adar strolled into the warehouse hangar, flanked by four secbots and a pair of uniformed officers.

Declan stepped forward to meet him. "Let us go, Dad. It's what you want, isn't it?"

"What I wanted," Howard bit out from between gritted jaws, "was to have a son who could take up the reins after me! And if I couldn't have that, at least one who knew our world and his proper place in it."

"I have no place in your world. Not anymore." Declan raised his hands to show he held no weapons. "Let us go, Dad."

Howard barked out a laugh that reverberated into echoing ugliness. "And have you gallivanting around the Intercolony for everyone to see?"

"I won't be trading on my name anymore. You don't have to worry about it."

Howard gestured for the secbots and Ops behind him to move forward. "I might believe that of your Adar point of honor, Caldyx, but what about your little friend?"

He put enough contempt into the word to make it an insult.

"Gemma has more honor than you'll ever have." Declan spoke calmly, though his father's voice kept rising.

"She's nothing better than a ten-credit whore! She's not even human anymore, she's mecho!" Howard's voice rose to an angry shriek like the grinding of rusty gears.

"She's what I am, Dad," Declan said calmly. "And neither of us is worth your disgust."

Howard trembled with the force of his rage, and his once handsome face purpled. "I wanted to let you die on that operating table, rather than see you become this."

I saw Declan's shoulders twitch as the words must have struck him hard, but his voice was still calm when he replied. "I used to wish that same thing, Dad. But not anymore. Let us go."

"I can't!" Howard roared. "You'll ruin me!"

"It's too late for that," I told him. "You've ruined yourself. There are more witnesses than us, Howard. More people who know the truth."

"You think so?" He looked back at the officers who accompanied him. "I suppose you're right."

With a jerk of his head he motioned to the secbots. "Kill them."

We had no time to protest. Secbots have no free will, no morals, nothing but the programmed need to obey orders. They lifted their weapons and shot. The uniformed officers had no time even to cry out before they fell.

Eddie let out a hoarse cry, then launched himself toward Howard. "You son of a bitch!"

"Him, too," Howard said almost casually.

Eddie, unlike our doomed peers, was prepared. He dodged out of the way and avoided the secbots' shots. One winged by me close enough for me to feel its heat.

"You can't just kill everyone who goes against you!" Declan cried.

Now it was the father who was calm against the son's agitation. "I can," he said. "And I will. I will do whatever is needed to keep the Adar name unsullied."

I surprised even myself with how swiftly I moved. I pushed my legs into a combination jump/run that put me next to Howard in a heartbeat.

"I can kill you," I said. "And I don't need a lasergun to do it, either."

"You could," he replied calmly, with a serene smile. "But you won't. You're not bred to it. You're not meant for it."

He was right, at least on the latter two accounts. Whether I would or not, neither of us would discover, because at that momen Kaelyn, startled into flight by Howard's outburst, ran toward the shelter of a stack of crates waiting to be loaded on the ship. The secbots turned toward her, their jointed arms each lifting identical laserguns.

"Shoot that freak!" Howard ordered.

"No!" The shout burst from my throat with the force of a bullet.

Kaelyn froze, eyes wide, wings for once stilled in shock. A breeze from the open hangar door lifted the silk of her hair away from her face, highlighting the lovely, alien features that so incensed Howard Adar.

I didn't have time to think, I just reacted. I flipped myself forward onto my hands and kicked my legs over my head. Once, twice, I flipped end over end to end up between my daughter and those who sought to cause her harm. I stood just in time to shield her from the shot that hit me in the chest and would have hit her in the head.

Instant, blinding agony ripped through me, and I went to my knees. I pushed her down behind me, still shielding her, and the second shot took me in the right shoulder.

Kaelyn scrabbled on hands and knees behind the shelter of the crates. I sank to the ground, willing away the pain, trying to no avail to force my body to respond. Declan moved so fast that to my pain-dimmed vision he seemed to blur.

He kicked the gun from the closest secbot and sent it hurtling to the floor, where it skittered along the cracked pavement and disappeared beneath the ship. Without stopping, he jammed a fist into the secbot's optic center and ripped out its eyes, complete with dangling, sparking wires.

Eddie leaped on the other bot's back and tore away the control panel at the back of its neck. The bot swung at the waist and tried to shake him off, but Eddie didn't stop until he'd torn out the handful of wires that made up the bot's communication system.

I couldn't black out, no matter how much my body wanted to. The pain which should have sent me spiraling into darkness stabbed me into a state of almost hyper lucidity. As it was, I heard every word, saw every action.

As though oblivious to the fight going on around him, Howard stepped toward where I lay on the dirty floor. The haze of pain that wouldn't let me pass out seemed to line him in brightness, while Eddie and Declan's struggle in the background to subdue the secbots blurred.

"You'd sacrifice yourself for that thing?" Howard asked me, his face showing his incredulity. "That inhuman creature? You'd die for that freak?"

"She is my child, and I would die for her, yes." Speaking took a great effort. Blood burbled to my lips, bringing with it a taste like rust. I swam against the tide of pain, unable to simply give up and let it take me. "Too bad you'll never know the depth of that love."

"You pity me?" Howard loomed over me, his features so familiar to Declan's, yet so foreign. "You mecho, you freak of nature? You dare to pity me?"

"I think you deserve my pity," I tried to say, but nothing came but a whisper and a froth of copper on my tongue.

Now, at last, the red glimmer of unconsciousness flickered at the edges of my vision. My sight narrowed, until all I saw was Howard's face, his shoulder as he reached into his pocket, his hand as he brought up a weapon of his own. And then, finally, the dark eye of the gun as he aimed it at my head.

I waited for the end, and it didn't come. Howard stiffened, his eyes widened, his arms flung out like a startled infant's. A hole appeared, black around the edges and red inside, in his chest. Daylight glimmered through it for a brief moment, and then he fell.

He hit the floor beside me, and the dust kicked up from his landing burned my eyes. I saw Declan through the blur, bending next to his father, and the almost reverent way he slid his hand over Howard's eyes to close them in unending sleep.

"I'm sorry, Dad," I heard him say, then felt the whisper of his breath against my bloodstained lips as he kissed me. "You'll be fine," he said. "I promise."

EPILOGUE

The sun was bright enough I had to shade my eyes against it when I looked out over the beach. Golden sand covered my feet. The breeze tangled my hair, now the color of a Shaddran sunset.

"Not too far out!" I cried to Kaelyn as she dipped and dove in the waves. Her wings gave her natural buoyancy, and in the gentle waters it would be nearly impossible for her to drown, but I didn't like to leave anything to chance.

Her laughter came to me on the salt breeze, and the sound of it filled my heart with a joy so fierce it took my breath away.

We'd made it, the four of us, to Shaddra, where the sun always shone and the drinks were always cold. Declan's Intercolony Credit account had been emptied to provide us with this moderate cottage, our clothes, our food, and the down payment on a small tourist pub Eddie had discovered was his true calling. Already my former partner had tanned as dark as the natives, and I was certain there'd be a bonding ceremony soon. Scores of tittering, simpering maidens flocked around him all the time, but he had eyes only for U'Elian, a dark haired beauty with a kind nature who already had a young son.

"I will watch the children," U'Elian said to me now, as her boy R'Etan leaped into the surf with Kaelyn. She spoke to me in softly accented English, though I'd been learning Shaddran. "They'll be fine. Why not go inside and rest for awhile?"

She lowered herself gracefully to the sand, her bright tunic puddled around her knees. "It will give me pleasure to watch them play,

G'Emma."

I nodded and stretched to clear my back of its kinks. My recovery from the wounds had been complicated by infection from lack of appropriate medical care. I'd won against the persistent fevers, aided by Shaddra's lovely weather and nutritious food. I still tired easily, however, and an afternoon rest would be very welcome.

"Thanks, U'Elian." I tried the words in Shaddran, and was rewarded with her pleased grin.

"I think perhaps there's a love match there." She nodded toward the children scampering in the water. "You start preparing her dowry now, yes?"

I laughed at the thought, but couldn't deny it pleased me to think Kaelyn could find a life here. Love, someday. Happiness. Yes, that idea pleased me very much.

"My E'Ddie, he works late tonight, serving dinner to tourists." U'Elian laughed. "I will take K'Aelyn tonight, to play with R'Etan. You have the night to…rest."

Her grin told me she knew there'd be little rest involved if Declan and I had the cottage to ourselves. Adjusting to life as a family had been difficult in ways I'd never imagined when Kaelyn and I shared the apartment in Newcity.

I stifled a yawn with the back of my hand, and couldn't stop from rubbing my eyes. "I think I will go in and take a nap, after all. I'm tired."

U'Elian raised her thin brow ridges until her oval eyes widened. "You're not sleeping enough at night, yes?" Then she laughed. "Ahh. My E'Ddie is much the same."

"I'm glad he found you," I told her. "He deserves a good woman."

She inclined her head. "He is a good man. As is your D'Eclan."

I though about Declan working with Eddie. "He's never had to work before. I think he's happy to have something to be proud of."

"You should be proud of him, G'Emma. He and my E'Ddie have made a success of that broken down tourist trap. Made it lovely."

"They have, haven't they?" I had to smile at the thought. "They really have."

I yawned again, harder this time, and stretched. "Kaelyn!"

She turned in her play. "Yes, my Gemma?"

"Do you want to spend the night with R'Etan and U'Elian tonight?"

Her squeal of delight was answer enough. I left the children splashing and playing under U'Elian's watchful gaze, and went inside the cottage. Inside was dim and cool, with ceiling fans and strategically opened windows to fan the breeze. The tile floor was chill on my bare feet as I padded into the kitchen to pour a drink of juice, and the hall to the bedroom smelled of the flowers that grew in abundance all over Shaddra.

I took off the light tunic I wore and slipped between sheets as fresh and sweet as sunshine could make them. The bed was soft, and I was sleepy, and in moments I had passed into sleep. I didn't dream.

I woke to a light touch along my arm, and Declan's weight sank onto the bed. Disoriented, I sat up, expecting darkness. Late afternoon sun slanted through the shuttered windows in bars of gold against the dark light tile floor.

"Hey." He stroked my hair. "How are you feeling?"

I stretched until the tiny bones along my spine crackled. "Good."

He touched my cheek, softly. I leaned into his touch and pressed a kiss to his palm.

"K is spending the night with U'Elian and R'Etan." The words left my mouth in a throaty whisper that was meant to be an invitation. "We have the whole house to ourselves."

He tossed me that sexy grin that had so captivated me the first time I saw him. "Let's see what we can do about that."

He shucked off the loose cotton trousers he wore. I took a long look at him, this man I'd grown to love. His firm, smooth chest. The line of hair tracing down his belly to the thicker patch at his crotch. The length of his erection stretched and rose at my gaze. His face flushed, and he slid into bed next to me.

Declan's mouth found the sensitive spot at the base of my neck as his hands slid up to cup my breasts. I arched against him as his fingertips found the scar tissue over my left breast. His touch there made me shiver.

"Does that hurt?" He whispered.

I shook my head. "Not anymore."

Seeing him stand before me had aroused me. Looking wasn't enough. I had to touch him, feel him, taste him. I moved to my knees and pushed him back gently against the pillows. I pressed my mouth along the firmness of his muscled chest, browned from the tropical sun, and brushed my cheeks with the softness of his pubic hair.

I took his cock into my mouth with a sigh he echoed. His hands found my hair and tangled there briefly. This was how we'd begun, what seemed so long ago, and the memory of that first encounter filled my mind now as I slid my tongue along the rim of his penis.

Declan's hips bucked a little beneath me as I took him inside my mouth again and sucked softly, then harder. Without stopping my rhythmic suckling, I turned onto my side and snuggled more comfortably along his body, so my thighs were close to his face.

My own hips jerked as his tongue sought my heated center. His hands cupped my buttocks, and he pulled me closer to slide my legs apart and reach my inner folds with his lips.

"I love the way you taste." The murmur against my flesh sent a burst of sensation tearing through me. "So sweet."

All at once, he pushed me until I rolled to my back. He turned so we no longer lay head to foot. He kissed my thighs, the curve of my belly, my taut nipples, then found my mouth with his. I parted my legs and he lay between them, his penis nestled in the slickness of my arousal. He moved his erection against my engorged clitoris. Slowly. Maddeningly slowly. His weight pressed me into the bed, his hands pinned my wrists above my head, and he continued to kiss every part of me his mouth could reach. All the while he stroked me with small, controlled movements of his hips.

A cry rose to my lips, and he took it with his mouth. With every stroke the tip of him nudged at my opening. I wanted him inside me, ached for him to slide into me, and he refused. My thighs shuddered with a climax that danced just out of my reach. I lifted my hips against him, but he moved away before I came.

"Say my name," he whispered. "I want to hear you say it."

"Declan," came my whispered reply, and he captured my mouth again.

He groaned when he finally thrust into me, and released my wrists. My arms went around him, and my hands smoothed his sweat-damp back. My hands found the clenching mounds of his buttocks, and I cupped him, urging him to love me harder, faster, deeper.

"Gemma."

"I love you, Declan." I kissed his chin, his chest, the curve of his jaw, his shoulder. "I love you!"

He shuddered as he thrust, and my climax built inside of me until I couldn't hold it back. I arched against him, meeting his thrusts with my own, and he slipped his arms beneath my back to cradle me closer as my orgasm began.

I've heard sexual climax referred to as a little death, and so it seemed to me that I died in Declan's arms just then, for the stars whirled around me and darkness pressed at my eyes. All the heaviness left my limbs until I floated, soared, swam, taken over by the unstoppable sensations pouring through my body. My clitoris felt as though it were on fire, bursts of white-hot pleasure radiating from it and through my entire body.

I heard myself cry his name again, and was surprised I was capable at that moment of speech at all. He answered me, and another burst of exquisite, agonizing pleasure ripped through me. Declan pressed his forehead to cheek to mine, and I sank into the scent of his hair as he spent himself inside of me.

Afterwards, we slept. I rose when the bars of golden light had turned to silver, and night fell across the beach. I went to the private balcony overlooking the sea and let the wind toss my hair and fill my nose with the scent of freedom.

To my right and across the small courtyard, I saw a light in the cottage Eddie and U'Elian shared. Inside I saw my friend and his lover tucking light covers around the children who made all our lives complete. I looked back to the sea, silver gilt moonlight shining on its waves. The sound of the waves spoke to me of dreams fulfilled and wishes granted.

I listened for awhile and let the peace of its song fill me. Then I blew a kiss through the window beyond to my sleeping child, and I went inside to dream next to the man I loved.

MEGAN HART

Megan Hart began her writing career in grammar school when she plagiarized a short story by Ray Bradbury. She soon realized that making up her own stories was better than copying other people's, and she's been writing ever since.

Megan's award-winning short fiction has appeared in such diverse publications as *Hustler*, *On Our Backs* and *The Reaper*. Her novels include every genre of romance, from historical to steamy futuristic SF. In addition to her short erotic fiction for the Amber Kisses imprint, look for her other Amber Quill novels: *Riverboat Bride*, *Lonesome Bride*, *Convicted! and Love Match.*

Megan's current projects include a fantasy series, a futuristic trilogy and a dramatic suspense novel. Her dream is to have a movie made of every one of her novels, starring herself as the heroine and Keanu Reeves as the hero. Megan lives in the deep, dark woods of Pennsylvania with her husband and two monsters…er…children.

Learn more about Megan by visiting her website:
http://www.meganhart.com

*   *   *

Don't miss Lonesome Bride, by Megan Hart, available Winter, 2003, from Amber Quill Press, LLC

Mail-order bride Caitleen O'Neal assumes the man who arrives at the train station to pick her up is the man she's agreed to marry. After all, he introduces himself as Jed Peters, the name on the papers the preacher gave her to sign. When a night of unexpected lovemaking turns Jed surly instead of sappy, Caite can't understand why. Only when they finally reach the ranch in Lonesome, Montana, does Caite discover the reason for her lover's cold shoulder. He's Jed Peters, all right. Jed Junior, and the white-haired man standing next to the woman he's just wed is Jed's father…the man Caite has come all the way from Pennsylvania to marry…

AMBER QUILL PRESS, LLC
THE GOLD STANDARD IN PUBLISHING

QUALITY BOOKS
IN BOTH PRINT AND ELECTRONIC FORMATS

ACTION/ADVENTURE	SUSPENSE/THRILLER
SCIENCE FICTION	PARANORMAL
MAINSTREAM	MYSTERY
ROMANCE	FANTASY
EROTICA	HORROR
HISTORICAL	WESTERN
YOUNG ADULT	NON-FICTION

AMBER QUILL PRESS, LLC
http://www.amberquill.com